Dear Reader,

Give me a choice betw[...] walking barefoot over [...] every time. It's just so [...] to say. I haven't lived in exotic places or done exotic things. I've lived in California for over twenty years now, most of them spent married to a really terrific guy who makes my life complete.

I have more hobbies than you can shake a stick at, assuming you had a stick you wanted to shake. I like to cook, especially to bake. If there's a needlecraft I haven't tried, it's only because I haven't heard of it yet. My current passion is quilting, but I also cross-stitch and knit. I collect dolls and dress them—the fancier and more intricate the garment the better. I love to garden, though I don't have as much time for it as I'd like. My reigning passion is writing, of course. Give me a notebook and pen and I can occupy myself for hours.

When I was asked to write *Cullen's Child*, my first response was, 'Me?' After all, I'm not anybody's mother, unless you count my very spoiled calico cat, and I think she considers me more slave than parent.

Then my editor told me the theme for the book was babies. Who can resist a baby? Who'd want to? So I thought up a story about a woman who thinks she has a very good reason for resisting a particular baby, and I put a baby smack-dab in the middle of her life. I hope you enjoy reading the end result as much as I enjoyed writing it.

Dallas Schulze

DALLAS SCHULZE

loves books, old movies, her husband and her cat, not necessarily in that order. She's a sucker for a happy ending, and her writing has given her an outlet for her imagination. Dallas hopes that readers have half as much fun with her books as she does! She has more hobbies than there is space to list them, but is currently working on a doll collection. Dallas loves to hear from her readers, and you can write to her at PO Box 241, Verdugo City, CA 91046, USA.

Dallas has a new novel in our Silhouette Sensation series in August 2003; look out for *Lovers and Other Strangers*.

Cullen's Child

DALLAS SCHULZE

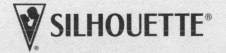

*Silhouette and Colophon are registered trademarks of
Harlequin Books S.A., used under licence.*

*First published in Great Britain 1995. This edition 2003.
Silhouette Books, Eton House, 18-24 Paradise Road,
Richmond, Surrey TW9 1SR*

© Dallas Schulze 1994

ISBN 0 373 60113 1

54-0603

*Printed and bound in Spain
by Litografia Rosés S.A., Barcelona*

Chapter One

A baby had never been part of the bargain.

Darcy Logan's expression was grim as she stared out the car window at the rain-washed scenery. The weather matched her mood, bleak and gray. She'd never been to Washington before and she hadn't seen anything yet to make her regret that lack. Oh, it was green and lush all right, but in the week since she and Cullen had arrived, she hadn't gotten more than a glimpse of the sun. It had been raining when they'd landed at the airport. It had been raining when they'd attended Susan Roberts's funeral and it had continued to rain in the five days since then. She was starting to think it never did anything else.

Of course, the weather was appropriate, considering the event that had brought them here. Cullen's sister had been two years short of her fortieth birthday when she died from cancer, leaving behind a six-month-old baby girl.

Darcy shivered. She'd never met Susan but her heart ached for what the other woman must have gone through. How terrible to be facing your own death when you should have been dealing with 2:00 a.m. feedings and diaper rash.

Cullen had taken his sister's death hard, she thought, glancing at him. Grief had carved lines that bracketed his mouth and had left a dulled sheen in his eyes. He hadn't been sleeping. She knew that because she hadn't been, either. Especially not the last couple of days since Cullen had told her that Susan had left her baby in his care.

Darcy's first reaction had been disbelief. And when Cullen had made it clear that he had every intention of fulfilling his sister's request, panic had taken over, closing her throat and making her heart pound.

"I owe it to her," he'd said before she could get out any of the words of denial.

"Don't make any quick decisions." She was amazed by how level her voice was. You'd never know that she felt like screaming her denial to the world.

"There's no decision to make. Susan made me the baby's guardian. She trusted me to do what's right for her."

"That doesn't necessarily mean that *you* have to raise her yourself," Darcy had protested reasonably. "Susan trusted you to make the right decision for her baby, but that could mean that somebody else—"

"There is no one else."

The flat statement had made her feel like an animal in a trap.

"What about your parents? Susan lived with them. She must have trusted them. They're the baby's grandparents. They might welcome a chance to raise her."

"No." Cullen had turned away from the window of their hotel room and looked at her, his eyes bleak. "The last thing she would have wanted was for my parents to raise her baby. That's why Susan made me her guardian, because she knew I'd never let that happen.''

Darcy had stared at him, bewilderment and panic churning inside her. ''But you said she lived with them.''

''Because they made sure she was incapable of doing anything else,'' Cullen had said bitterly.

''I don't understand.''

''You will when you meet my parents. I don't think I can explain it to you before then.'' He'd picked his denim jacket up off the bed. ''Let's get some lunch.''

And Darcy, too shaken to pursue the discussion, had followed him from the room and eaten a meal that could have been sawdust for all the attention she'd paid to it.

That had been yesterday and now, here they were, about to pick up Cullen's niece. About to destroy the happiness she'd found these past few months.

''This is it.'' Cullen's flat announcement dragged her out of her thoughts. He pulled the car over next to the curb.

Darcy glanced at the house, seeing a neat, two-story brick building bracketed by tidy flower beds. The white trim extended to the perfectly centered wooden porch, which housed a metal glider covered in pastel floral cushions. All in all a pleasant, if not particularly inspired, picture. Certainly nothing to cause the bleak expression in Cullen's eyes. He couldn't have looked more grim if the view had been a bombed-out inner city block rather than a plainly affluent suburban neighborhood.

She struggled with the urge to reach out and

smooth the lines from beside his mouth. Despite the
fact that they'd been lovers for eight months and had
lived together for the last five of those months, she
wasn't sure she had a right to try to soothe his pain.

They'd met at a party given by a mutual friend. By
the end of the evening Cullen had persuaded her to
go out with him, despite the fact that she'd avoided
even the most shallow of entanglements for the past
six years. But she'd been alone so long and he'd refused to take no for an answer. He'd made her laugh,
something she'd done precious little of lately. So
she'd agreed to go out with him, telling herself that
her agreement had nothing to do with the fact that he
made her heart beat a little too fast.

A week later she'd found herself in bed with him.
Three months after that, when he'd found out that her
apartment building was about to be turned into con-
dos, Cullen had suggested that she move in with him.
She'd refused, feeling that odd little flutter of panic
that came with the thought of getting close to someone again. But he'd pointed out that she'd spent every
weekend at his place, not to mention two or three
nights a week. She was practically living there, anyway. Besides, everyone knew that two could live
cheaper than one. Think of the money they'd save.

It was a silly argument. Neither one of them had
any real financial worries. Cullen and his partner ran
a very successful construction firm in Santa Barbara.
Darcy's salary as loan officer in a small bank might
not put her in the *Fortune 500* but she made enough
to be comfortable. Living together had nothing to do
with saving money and they both knew it.

Still, she'd let herself be persuaded. The truth was, Cullen filled up some of the empty spaces in her heart. He was like a fire on a cold, snowy night and she couldn't resist the urge to draw closer to him, to warm herself on his heat.

Five months later her heart was still turning over in her chest every time she looked at him. Not that it came as any surprise. Cullen Roberts had probably been stirring heart palpitations in women since he'd reached puberty.

Darcy looked at him, trying to define what it was about him that made him so impossibly attractive. His dark brown hair was worn just long enough and shaggy enough to make a woman want to run her fingers through it. His eyes were a clear, vivid blue and always seemed to be laughing, even when his mouth was solemn. And when he did smile... Well, a smart woman would run for cover, Darcy thought. She'd always considered herself a smart woman but she hadn't run far enough or fast enough.

But he wasn't smiling now. He was staring out the windshield, his hands still gripping the wheel, his mouth tight, his eyes bleak. Darcy noticed that he still hadn't looked at his parents' house, the house where he'd grown up.

"It's a very pretty house," she said when the silence had stretched to uncomfortable lengths. "Looks like a nice neighborhood to grow up in."

Looks like a great place for a motherless baby, she wanted to say, but didn't.

"I haven't been back here in seventeen years," he

said, finally turning to look at the house. "When I left, I swore I'd never come back."

The uncharacteristic bitterness in his voice startled her. Since he'd never mentioned them, she'd assumed he wasn't close to his parents. And the fact that they hadn't exchanged so much as a word at his sister's funeral had confirmed the accuracy of that assumption. But the old anger that roughened his voice still caught her off guard.

"I guessed there were…problems between you and your parents," she said hesitantly. "But seventeen years is a long time."

"Not long enough. I wouldn't have stayed as long as I did if it hadn't been for Susan." The name cracked in the middle, his mouth twisting with pain as he thought of his dead sister.

Darcy touched the back of his hand where it was clenched on the steering wheel. This was the first time either of them had faced any sort of personal crisis and she was uncertain about offering him comfort. She'd barely known he had a sister until the early-morning call last week that had told him of her death.

"I should have come back for her," he said abruptly. "I shouldn't have let her stay here."

"She wasn't a child, Cullen. She was four years older than you are. If she chose to stay, there was nothing you could do about it."

"You don't know Susan. She isn't—wasn't," he corrected painfully, "strong the way you are. She didn't have the ability to stand up for herself. She'd stand up for me but never for herself."

Strong like her? God, did he really believe she was

strong? She must be a better actress than she'd realized, Darcy thought bitterly, if she'd kept him from
seeing just how weak she really was.

"Still, she was thirty-eight years old, Cullen. And
she had a job at a day-care center. She didn't have to
live with your parents. She could have moved out."

Cullen was already shaking his head. He shot her
a look that said she didn't understand.

"You don't know my parents." Without another
word, he pushed open his car door and got out.

Darcy fumbled with her seat belt, aware that her
fingers were trembling. She had to talk to him before
he saw his parents. Ever since he'd told her what was
in Susan's will, she'd been trying to find the words
to say what needed to be said. But they needed to be
the right words, just the right tone of voice.

She finally mastered the unfamiliar latch just as
Cullen pulled open her car door. It was more misting
than raining, just damp enough to be annoying but
not enough to warrant an umbrella. Darcy could feel
the moisture settling on her hair as she slid out of the
rental car. Cullen's hand came under her elbow,
steadying her. Just as he'd been doing since they'd
met—steadying her, taking care of her. God, she
couldn't lose that now. And she would if she couldn't
talk him out of this. She put her hand on his arm and
tilted her head back to look up at him, ignoring the
dampness.

"You know, Cullen, I've been thinking about this
situation." Yes, that was good. She sounded calm, no
trace of the screaming panic she felt inside showed in
her voice. "I know you want to honor Susan's wishes,

but have you considered the possibility that your
niece might be better off staying with your parents?''
She saw denial flicker in his eyes and hurried on before he could interrupt. ''After all, even if *you* had
problems with them, this is the only home she's
known. Maybe it wouldn't be such a good idea to
take her away from all that's familiar. The lawyer said
that your parents want to raise her and this is a beautiful neighborhood. The schools are probably terrific
and—''

He put his finger against her mouth, stilling the
tumble of words. ''I know we haven't really discussed
any of this, Darcy, and I'm probably not being fair to
you to make decisions like this without your input.
But Susan made me Angie's guardian and I'm not
leaving without her.''

''I'm just trying to think of what's best for the
baby,'' she said. She felt her cheeks heat with shame.
*Liar. You're thinking of what's best for you. You
know what's going to happen if he brings this baby
home. You're going to lose him.* ''Are you sure she
wouldn't be better off with her grandparents?''

''You haven't met my parents,'' he said again, and
there was something in his tone that told her it would
be a waste of breath to continue the argument.

''What about the baby's father?'' She was clutch-
ing at straws, but when you were drowning, it was
worth grabbing at any possibility.

''The lawyer said he wants nothing to do with the
baby.''

''He might feel that way now. But that doesn't
mean he won't change—''

"He's married and has three kids, Darcy. In the letter Susan left me, she said not to contact him, that he knew about the baby and had offered her money but he wanted no actual involvement."

"Oh." Darcy spared a moment of sympathy for Cullen's sister, for the hurt she must have felt. But she couldn't help but feel a wave of panic on her own behalf. Cullen wouldn't leave the baby with his parents and the baby's father wanted no part of her. That didn't leave very many options.

"Don't look so upset, honey." Cullen smiled down at her.

"I'm not upset," she lied.

Darcy didn't know what he read in her eyes, surely not the fear she felt. She'd spent years learning to control her expression, learning to reveal only what she chose. But whatever Cullen saw, it made his face soften, one side of his mouth kicking up in a lopsided version of the smile that had persuaded her to go to bed with him barely a week after they'd met.

He smoothed one finger over the curve of her cheekbone. "We'll work everything out, Darcy. I promise. Once the three of us get back to Santa Barbara, we'll take time to sort it all out."

The three of us. Words right out of a nightmare.

Darcy couldn't force a smile but she managed to nod. Apparently it was enough to satisfy Cullen because he bent to drop a quick kiss on her cold mouth.

"Thanks, sweetheart."

Linking his hand with hers, he led the way up the cement walkway. Darcy felt like a prisoner walking to her doom. These past eight months with Cullen had been the happiest of her life. And unless he changed his mind about letting his parents raise his sister's child, it was all going to come to an end.

Cullen could feel Darcy's tension in the hand he held. He knew she was upset, knew that he was probably being unfair in making a unilateral decision on such a major issue. They should discuss the impact a baby would have on their lives, talk about what kind of changes it would mean, how they would deal with those changes. He should ask her how she felt about bringing a baby into the life they'd built together.

He *should* do all those things, but at the moment he couldn't get past the basic facts: Susan was dead and she'd left her baby to him. She'd trusted him with the most precious thing in her life. And nothing—not even Darcy—was going to keep him from fulfilling that trust.

Darcy would understand, he told himself. Once she'd met his parents, she'd understand why there had been no choices to be made about this, why he hadn't consulted her, asked her what she thought.

There was a knot in his chest as he stepped onto the porch. He'd been a scared, angry seventeen-year-old when he'd left home. That was half a lifetime ago. At thirty-four, he was a successful businessman, with money in the bank. He owned his own home, two cars and half a boat. And since meeting Darcy, his personal life was on track. He was, by any standards you cared to apply, successful.

So why was he standing in front of his parents' door with a knot in his stomach and the feeling that he'd failed in some indefinable but significant way?

It was a feeling that had been all too familiar when he was growing up, a feeling he'd thought he'd left behind him when he'd left home.

Darcy tugged on the hand he was holding, making him realize that he was crushing her fingers.

"Sorry." He released her. "I'm a little uptight, I guess."

"It's been a rough week." She reached up to touch the lines of strain that bracketed his mouth. Cullen was momentarily soothed by the concern in her eyes.

He brushed his fingers across her cheek. Even after all these months, he sometimes found it hard to believe that she was really his. He'd wanted her from the moment he'd seen her. He'd gone to his friend's barbecue only because he had nothing better to do, thinking he could always leave early if he wanted. Darcy had been standing in a patch of sunlight, her hair so pure a gold it almost hurt to look at it. He'd wangled an introduction, taken one look at the smile in her pale, almost crystalline gray eyes and fallen like a ton of bricks.

Darcy's light shiver brought him back to the present, back to the task at hand, which was getting Susan's baby out of his parents' house. He gave Darcy a quick, strained smile that didn't quite reach his eyes.

"This shouldn't take long."

Cullen ignored the doorbell and rapped his knuckles against the smooth oak of the door. He was aware of Darcy glancing at him, her eyes curious, and knew that she must have a lot of questions. He'd never talked about his family with her, so she could have no idea how he felt about this homecoming. But then, he didn't know much about her family, either. Maybe he should ask—

The sound of footsteps on the other side of the door made him break off the thought. The sharp tap of high heels on polished oak floors. His mother. The only woman he'd ever known who wore high heels at home. And then the door was opening and, for the first time in seventeen years, he and his mother stood face-to-face.

She hadn't changed much. There was more gray threaded through her medium brown hair, a few more lines on her forehead. But her eyes were the same—looking at him, measuring him, finding him wanting. Just as she had when he was a boy.

"Cullen." Maeve Roberts's greeting was flat and emotionless.

"Mother." He was so tense that his neck ached.

"Come in." Her eyes, the same deep blue as her son's, flickered over Darcy. "Both of you."

Darcy felt the tension in Cullen as they stepped across the threshold. Not exactly a fatted calf kind of welcome, she thought.

The interior of the house was as neat as the exterior. Light oak wood floors, creamy white walls, a few delicately shaded watercolors on the walls—all very pale and restful. Not the kind of decor one associated with children. She felt her hopes of Cullen leaving the baby here slip a little more.

"Nothing's changed," Cullen said, half to himself. "This is just the way it looked when I was a kid."

"Your father and I enjoy our home," Maeve said

over her shoulder. "We've seen no reason to change it."

She led the way into the living room, which was decorated with the same lack of color as the entryway. In here, the floor was covered with a plush carpet in a pale fawn color. Guaranteed to show every bit of dirt, Darcy thought. She resisted the urge to glance behind herself to make sure she wasn't leaving footprints.

"Cullen is here, William." Maeve made the announcement in the same flat tone of voice with which she'd greeted her son.

There was a strong resemblance between William Roberts and his son, Darcy saw as the older man set aside the paper he'd been reading and rose from his chair. It was there in the shape of his face, in the tobacco brown of his hair, still visible through the liberal sprinkling of gray. His eyes were blue, also, though a paler shade than his wife's and son's.

But where Cullen's eyes usually sparkled with life and his mouth always seemed to hover on the edge of a smile, there was a stillness about his father's face, a tightness about his mouth that made it difficult to imagine him smiling at all.

"Cullen." He nodded as if greeting an acquaintance he hadn't seen for some time.

"Dad." Cullen's greeting was just as cool. "This is Darcy Logan. Darcy, my parents."

Darcy murmured an acknowledgment, aware of William's cool eyes skimming over her and dismissing her.

"Are you my son's mistress?" Maeve asked in the

same tone she might have used to ask if Darcy liked jam on her toast.

Darcy's mouth gaped in shock. She was at a loss for an answer. *His mistress?* Did anyone actually think in those terms anymore? Cullen's hand squeezed hers. In warning? In support?

"Darcy and I have been living together for the last five months," Cullen said. "Not that it's any of your business."

"I think we have a right to know what kind of moral atmosphere you're taking our grandchild into," Maeve said, pressing her lips together.

"No, actually, you don't." Cullen's tone was almost pleasant. "Susan's will gave me sole custody of her daughter."

"If she'd lived longer, Susan would have changed her mind," William said heavily. "She'd begun to realize the sin she'd committed, bearing a child out of wedlock as she had."

"I'm sure you helped her see that. I'm sure you made sure she knew every minute of every day just what a crime she'd committed."

"Unlike you, Susan had some understanding of the importance of strong moral behavior." William didn't so much as glance in Darcy's direction, but she knew the words were a reference to her presence. Clearly, as far as Cullen's parents were concerned, the fact that he had a mistress—good Lord, had they really used that term?—made it clear that Cullen didn't share his sister's understanding.

"Where's the baby?" Though she could feel the anger in him, Cullen's tone was level.

"She's upstairs." Maeve glanced at her husband. "We feel it would be better if she stayed with us. Clearly, you're in no position to be taking on the rearing of a child."

"Bring her down."

"Though your father and I didn't ask for this burden, we feel it's our duty to—"

"Are you going to bring her down or should I go up and get her?"

The steel in Cullen's voice cut through his mother's words. Glancing at his face, Darcy suppressed a shiver. She hoped never to see that look turned in her direction.

"Don't speak to your mother in that tone," William said sternly. "We've decided the child would be better off under our care. If you—"

"I don't give a damn what you've decided." Cullen's eyes blazed with an emotion perilously close to hate. "Susan made me the baby's guardian. If you want to argue with that, then you can do it in court."

"I see you haven't changed since you were a boy," William said, and the words were not intended as a compliment. "You're still overly emotional and thoughtless to a fault."

"You mean, I'm not a block of morally unimpeachable ice like the two of you. I'll take that as a compliment."

"You're thinking only of yourself here. You're not giving a thought to what's best for the child. If she stays with us, she'll have stability. She'll grow up with a firm understanding of right and wrong, with—"

''Without love, with no sense of self-worth,'' Cullen interrupted. ''You'll break her spirit the same way you broke Susan's, the way you tried to break mine. Only I was lucky enough to have Susan to love me, to push me out before you could destroy me the way you did her.'' He took a short step forward, using the advantage of an extra two inches of height to loom over the older man. ''Now, are you going to bring her baby down here or am I going to have to tear the goddamned house apart to find her?''

Cullen didn't raise his voice. He didn't have to. The cold rage in his eyes was threat enough. Darcy put her hand on his arm, half-afraid he might actually strike his father. His muscles were rigid as iron beneath her fingers. The silence stretched.

William looked away first, his pale eyes shifting to his wife. He nodded abruptly. ''Get her.''

Maeve's lips compressed. She glanced at Cullen and for an instant, Darcy saw some emotion flash through her eyes, something that could have been hatred. It was gone immediately, but the memory of it stayed in Darcy's mind, chilling her.

What kind of people were they that they could look at their son with such hatred, that they could talk about their recently deceased daughter having committed a terrible moral sin? Where was the grief they should have been feeling over Susan's death? The regret that their relationship with their only remaining child was such a shambles? Darcy shivered and drew her jade green jacket shut over the matching dress. It seemed colder in here than it did outside.

Maeve left the room at a measured pace, the skirt

of her neat, powder blue dress barely shifting as she moved. She was as tidy and soulless as the house, Darcy thought. No wonder Cullen was so determined to take charge of his niece. What must it have been like growing up in such a sterile, judgmental household? She'd spent less than ten minutes here and already felt chilled to the bone.

No one spoke while they waited. The tension that stretched between the two men was at odds with the pristine, colorless room. From the little she'd seen of them, Darcy suspected that Cullen's parents were strangers to strong emotions of any sort. Unless you considered feeling morally superior an emotion.

She heard the click of Maeve's heels in the hall and then the older woman walked into the room carrying a blanket-wrapped bundle. There was suddenly a hard knot in Darcy's chest, making it hard to breathe. She let her hand drop from Cullen's arm as he stepped forward to meet his mother.

Maeve hesitated a moment, her eyes meeting her son's. Whatever she read there apparently convinced her that further argument would be a waste of time. With a look of unconcealed dislike, she allowed him to take the baby from her arms.

Cullen showed none of the hesitancy Darcy might have expected from a man who had little or no experience with babies. His hold was secure, if a little awkward. She noticed that his hand was not quite steady as he eased the blanket back from the baby's face.

Uncle and niece stared at each other with identically colored blue eyes. The baby managed to work one hand free of the soft white blanket, waving it aimlessly in the air. She gurgled a greeting.

"Hello, little one." Cullen's facial expression was nothing short of captivated.

Baby Angie, with a wisdom far beyond her six months, solidified her position by rewarding him with a grin that crinkled her small face and revealed two tiny teeth. Cullen returned the grin and Darcy watched helplessly as his heart fell firmly into the infant's tiny hands.

Chapter Two

"Are you sure she's warm enough?" It was the second time Cullen had asked the question in the twenty minutes since they'd left his parents' house.

"She's wrapped in a blanket and the heater is on. Besides, it's damp but it's not that cold outside. This is Seattle not Siberia."

"Sorry." Cullen's smile was self-deprecating. "It's just that she's so little."

"Most babies are." Darcy flicked on a turn signal preparatory to making the turn into a supermarket parking lot. Baby Angie had come with a limited supply of basic necessities like diapers and formula. Clothes could wait until they got back to Santa Barbara, but the rest of it couldn't.

Once inside, they found the baby-food aisle easily enough, but the array of choices made Cullen's eyes glaze with fear. Taking pity on him, Darcy made a few quick choices, tossing items into a cart and trying to ignore the bundle in Cullen's arms, a feat considerably more difficult than she would have liked.

At the checkout counter, Cullen tried to hand Darcy the baby so he could get out his checkbook.

"No!" The refusal was automatic and held a panic-stricken note that made his eyebrows go up. She forced a smile. "I'll pay for it. I've already got my checkbook out." She waved it for emphasis.

"Okay."

She thought he gave her a questioning look, but the clerk chose that moment to admire Angie, who was peering over the edge of her blanket to offer that irresistible two-toothed smile. The clerk smiled fatuously. Cullen looked proud. Darcy kept her eyes resolutely turned away.

By the time they reached the hotel, the knot in her stomach had grown to roughly the size of a basketball and all she wanted was to lock herself in the bathroom with a full tub of hot water and not come out until her skin looked like a topographical map of the Sierras.

But when she mentioned the idea to Cullen, he looked as if she'd just threatened to abandon him in the middle of a jungle without so much as a can of bug repellent. He ran a construction company, for heaven's sake, she reminded herself. So how was it possible for him to look so utterly helpless holding a baby?

"I think she's wet," he said, sounding every bit as helpless as he looked.

"Babies do that. We bought plenty of disposable diapers." She pulled the box from one of the grocery sacks and set it on the bed.

To his credit, Cullen didn't ask her to do the job for him. He carried Angie over to the bed and laid her down, unwrapping her from her blanket with methodical care. Darcy told herself that she should get started filling the tub, but she didn't move. Cullen's hands looked huge as he fumbled with the series of tiny snaps that ran down each leg of Angie's pink romper.

The minute her legs were freed, Angie began kicking and waving her arms in the air. She opened her perfect rosebud mouth and squealed loud enough to wake the dead. Cullen jerked back as if she were a rattlesnake coiled to strike.

"What's wrong? Did I hurt her?"

"There's nothing wrong. She's just letting you know she's here."

"As if I hadn't noticed," he muttered, warily approaching his niece once more.

It took some effort, but he managed to remove both plastic pants and wet diaper. Angie kicked harder, apparently delighted to find herself bare bottomed. Cullen disposed of the wet diaper and pulled a new one from the box Darcy had helpfully opened.

Diaper in hand, he leaned over Angie.

Both her tiny legs churned like pistons.

He gave Darcy a questioning look as if she might know the trick for getting a six-month-old baby to hold still.

Darcy shrugged.

Looking grimly determined, Cullen turned back to his niece.

Ten minutes and three ruined diapers later, lines of defeat had appeared beside his mouth. His fingers were locked around diaper number four, the knuckles white with tension as he eyed his opponent. She grinned up at him, and babbled something that sounded suspiciously like "I win."

Darcy was torn between laughter and sympathy. A

heavy lock of dark hair tumbled onto his forehead. His eyes held a wild look generally only seen in trapped animals. There were damp patches on the underarms of his shirt, though the temperature in the room couldn't have been more than seventy degrees.

Darcy took pity on him. No matter how much she wanted to keep her distance, she couldn't stand by and watch him suffer. Not to mention that, at the rate he was going, they were going to run out of diapers long before they boarded their plane tomorrow morning.

"Let me try." She came forward and held out her hand for the diaper.

"I don't think she wants to wear a diaper," Cullen said as he handed it to her.

"She's just testing you to see who's the boss." She opened the diaper and set it on the bed next to the wiggling baby.

"*She* is," Cullen conceded immediately.

"Are you going to let yourself be bullied by a baby who probably doesn't even weigh as much as fifteen pounds?"

"Yes."

"Coward." She looked down at Angie, who waved her arms and babbled happily. Darcy couldn't help but grin back at her. She felt something loosen in her chest, like a key sliding into a lock that hadn't been turned in a very long time. But she didn't want to open that particular lock, she reminded herself. Not ever again.

"Your uncle is a coward," she told the baby.

"Imagine a grown man like him letting a little thing like you bully him."

Angie babbled and cooed as Darcy caught both her ankles in one hand and lifted her far enough to slide the diaper under her bottom. A minute later, the baby was diapered, and a clean romper tugged on over her wiggling body.

"How did you do that?" Cullen demanded suspiciously, as if he hadn't watched the entire operation.

"You just have to be firm and remember that you're bigger than she is."

"I was afraid I'd hurt her," he muttered, staring down at his niece.

"Not likely. Babies are tougher than—" The words caught in her throat, painful, as if she'd swallowed a fishhook.

"Than I think," Cullen finished for her, apparently seeing nothing odd in her abruptly ended sentence. "I guess they'd have to be or else the whole human race would be out of business. It's just that she's so little." He leaned down to touch Angie's hand and she promptly grabbed hold of his finger. "Look at how tiny her fingers are. And did you see her toes?"

"Yes." Darcy was pleased to hear how steady her voice was.

"It's incredible, isn't it?"

"Incredible," she said dully. Cullen glanced at her and she forced a quick smile as she turned toward the phone. "She'll probably be hungry soon. I'll call room service and see how we go about getting her formula heated up."

"And I wanted to call Sara and see if she'd be

willing to do some shopping for us tomorrow morning.''

''Shopping?'' Sara Randall was Cullen's secretary. Darcy had met her a few times and liked her.

''For baby stuff. You know, cribs and strollers and whatever babies need. She's got three grandchildren. She's bound to know what to buy.''

Darcy nodded and picked up the phone. ''Good idea.''

Shopping for baby furniture was right up there on her list of favorite things, right next to having a root canal or getting her hair died purple.

''I don't know what I'd have done without Susan.'' Cullen's voice was low, in deference to the baby sleeping in a crib provided by the hotel. ''She was the only thing that made life bearable when I was a kid.''

The two of them were lying in bed. Darcy was exhausted, physically and emotionally, yet sleep had never seemed less likely. It was obvious that Cullen felt the same.

''The two of you must have been close.'' She looked over at his profile. He'd drawn only the sheer inner drapes earlier and the light of a full moon shone through them, illuminating the room with pale clarity.

''We were. I would have run away from home long before I was seventeen if it hadn't been for Susan. I didn't want to leave her and I knew she wouldn't come with me.''

''Why? If things were so terrible, why did she stay?''

"It sounds melodramatic but I think they'd broken her spirit." Darcy heard the rustle as he shrugged. "I don't ever remember hearing a word of praise from either of my parents. From the time I was little, I was told what a failure I was, how I had to try harder to be worthy of the Lord's love. I remember thinking that I could do without His love if only *they'd* love me."

"They must have loved you." Darcy's protest was weak as she remembered the icy dislike with which they'd looked at him earlier.

"I don't think so. I'm not sure they even love each other. They're cold, soulless people, Darcy." There was no anger in his voice, only the flatness of someone stating a fact. "They never hugged us or told us we'd done a good job. If you got bad grades, you were sent to your room to contemplate your sins— their exact words—and they didn't speak to you for a week. If you got good grades, they never said a word. I think it would have been easier to deal with out and out anger. If they'd hit me, at least it would have been a reaction of some kind, an acknowledgment that they felt *something* for me."

"It sounds like a lonely way to grow up," Darcy said softly, her heart aching for the small boy he'd been.

"It would have been if it hadn't been for Susan. She was four when I was born and I think she was so desperate for someone to love and to love her that she practically adopted me as her own. She was always there for me, proud of me if I did something good, telling me I'd do better next time if things went wrong.''

"She sounds wonderful."

"She was the best," he said simply. "I kept in touch after I left. As soon as I was scraping out a living, I asked her to come live with me. She always put me off and I let her." There was bitter self-condemnation in his words.

"You couldn't make her leave, Cullen," Darcy said. She reached out hesitantly and touched his shoulder, feeling the knotted muscles there. "She made her own choices."

"I think she was afraid to leave them. Or maybe she was afraid she'd be intruding on my life."

"Maybe. But she still had to make her own choices. You can't beat yourself up because she didn't take you up on your offer to help her leave."

There was a long silence and she hoped Cullen was thinking about what she'd said. He couldn't hold himself responsible for the choices his sister had made. No one could force someone else to do what was best for them.

"She didn't tell me she was sick." There was a lost sound to the words that made Darcy's heart twist.

"She probably didn't want you to worry."

"If she'd told me she was sick, I would have been here for her."

"I know you would have." Darcy eased over, closing the gap between them.

"I talked to her a month ago and when I asked if she was all right, she said she was a little tired but that was all. I was in a hurry and I forgot to tell her I loved her.'' His voice was suspiciously thick.

"She knew, Cullen. I'm sure she knew." She could hardly get the words out past the lump in her throat.

Acting on instinct, she slid her arm under his neck and pulled him toward her. He was stiff for a moment, rejecting the comfort she was offering. The stiffness left him abruptly and his arms came around her in a convulsive movement.

"I didn't get to tell her goodbye."

His hold on her was painfully tight, but Darcy didn't protest. She stroked her hand over his thick, dark hair, offering him wordless comfort. There was little else she could do for him. Only time could heal his wounds.

And sometimes a wound was so deep that not even time could reach it. Her eyes were bleak as she stared over Cullen's head at the crib and the sleeping baby it held.

Any uneasiness that either of them might have felt the next morning over the intensely emotional scene of the night before was swallowed up by the hustle and bustle of getting ready to go to the airport. Angie was not a morning person and she announced this fact most emphatically.

Unfortunately there wasn't much that could be done about it, so the ride to the airport was made to the accompaniment of her protests. By the time they boarded the plane, she'd begun to regain the sunny nature she'd displayed the day before. At Darcy's suggestion, Cullen gave her a bottle to suck on as they took off and it seemed to do the trick because there were no more tears between Seattle and Santa Barbara.

In fact, she cooed her pleasure as she arrived at her new home. The adults, on the other hand, were more than a little the worse for the wear. After a week of emotional ups and down, the condo looked like paradise. As soon as Darcy got out of the car, she turned her face up to the sun, letting its warmth beat down on her.

But not even the California sun could warm her all the way through, she thought as Cullen got out of the car behind her with Angie cradled in his arms. His eyes met hers and she forced a smile. He had enough to deal with, what with his sister's death and suddenly finding himself with an infant to care for. He didn't need the additional pressure of her own personal demons.

Sara Randall had proved herself more than worth her weight in gold. She'd not only gone shopping for everything a baby could need, but she'd arranged to have everything delivered. Cullen's partner, Kiel Jackson, had provided a key to the condo and the two of them had set up the spare bedroom as a temporary nursery.

Tired as she was, Darcy welcomed their presence, especially Sara's. The older woman was more than happy to hold Angie and exclaim over what an extraordinary baby she was. In the fervor of her welcome, Darcy hoped her own lack of enthusiasm would be more easily overlooked. Not that she didn't agree that Angie was a remarkably beautiful and good-natured baby. It was just that she really didn't want to get close enough to notice such things.

She only had to get through tonight, she told herself, listening with half an ear as Kiel filled Cullen in on the business of the past week. Tomorrow she'd be going back to work and she wouldn't have to deal with the painful ache that twisted her heart every time she looked at Angie.

A little time and distance, that was all she needed to get things into perspective, to settle everything in her head. A few days and she'd find a way to deal with the situation. Not that there was much ''dealing'' to be done. She could either adjust to Angie's presence in her life—in *their* lives—or she could give Cullen up. And since she was unwilling to do the latter, then she'd have to find some way to cope with the former.

Darcy woke suddenly, her heart pounding, her skin chilled and damp. Bits of nightmare chased her from sleep, images too thin to catch yet that left her trembling with remembered fear. It had been a long time since she'd had this particular nightmare, but the aftermath was still familiar. She'd never been able to remember much about it except for the sound of a baby crying.

A shallow wail brought her upright in bed, her breath catching in her throat. Still foggy with sleep, for an instant it seemed that the nightmare had followed her into the waking world, just as she'd always been afraid it would. But when the wail came again, Darcy realized what it was. Angie.

It was a real flesh-and-blood baby crying, not the wraith of her nightmares. Darcy sagged, her breath gusting out of her on a half sob of relief. Angie cried again and she felt Cullen stir. She started to sink back down against the pillows. He'd take care of the baby, just as he'd been doing since they'd brought her home.

Another wail, this one with a lost, inquiring sound that had Darcy on her feet before the sound died down. She could no more ignore that cry than she could walk on water. It called out some deep maternal response that couldn't be denied.

The addition of a crib had turned the condo's spare bedroom into a nursery. A heavy oak dresser served both to store Angie's small wardrobe and act as a changing table. The double bed had been shoved into a corner to make room for the crib, a stroller, a car seat, and a box of toys. Angie hadn't brought much with her by way of material possessions, but Cullen had made up for that lack.

Angie wailed again as Darcy entered the room, the sound dying down to a series of sad little whimpers. Ignoring the clutter illuminated by the night-light, Darcy walked across the room and stopped beside the crib. Angie was lying on her back, her face crumpled with tears.

"What's the matter?" Darcy asked softly.

At the sound of her voice, the baby's eyes flew open. She stared up at Darcy for a moment as if pondering her presence. In the week since they'd brought Angie home, Darcy had managed to keep her distance for the most part. After considerable thought, she'd decided that that was her only option.

It was a ridiculously simple strategy but it had worked fairly well so far. She simply did her best to be elsewhere when Angie needed attention. There were times when it hadn't worked out that way, of course. If Cullen was showering or on the phone and the baby needed something, Darcy didn't ignore her. Not only would that have been unfair to the baby but it would have made her aversion to his niece obvious to Cullen. The last thing she wanted was him questioning her feelings about Angie and babies in general.

Making up her mind, Angie lifted her arms in a clear demand to be picked up, babbling something that could probably be interpreted as "What took you so long?" Darcy wondered if Angie thought she was her mother. Or did she remember Susan, wonder at her abrupt disappearance?

Angie babbled again, jerking her arms impatiently, but Darcy hesitated. She'd done her best to avoid holding the baby if she could. It hurt too much. It was stupid really. It wasn't as if she hadn't held other babies in the past few years.

Last year, there had been a mini baby boom at the bank and it seemed as if someone was bringing in a new infant every other week. She'd held each of them, admired them and had managed to hold the memories at bay. But Angie was different. Angie wasn't just in her life for a moment. Angie was here to stay and it would be so easy to let herself forget, to let herself get too close. That wouldn't be fair to either of them.

Cullen had been so busy adapting to his abrupt introduction to fatherhood that he hadn't had time to notice anything else. He'd even been letting his partner, Kiel Jackson, run their construction company so he could devote himself completely to easing Angie's transition to her new life. But eventually things would slow down a little and he'd realize that she treated his adorable niece much as she would a python, interesting enough to look at but something from which to keep her distance. And then he'd want to know why she was so careful to keep Angie at arm's length.

And just what was she going to say? "Sorry, I just don't like babies?" Or did she tell him the truth and risk seeing the look in his eyes change to contempt? The thought caused a stabbing pain in her chest.

Angie's smile faded at the delay and she whimpered, her lower lip quivering pathetically. Darcy moved automatically to stop the howl that was sure to follow that look. Cullen hadn't had a decent night's sleep since they'd got home from Seattle. If she could help him sleep a little longer by changing a wet diaper and settling the baby back in her crib, she'd do it.

She'd held Angie before. So the solid weight of her wasn't the shock it had been the first time. Still, Darcy's heart jerked a little as she felt Angie's small body settle into her arms. She closed her eyes a moment, her breath catching on the sharp pain in her chest.

Swallowing hard, she opened her eyes and drew a deep breath, forcing her thoughts to the here and now.

She carried Angie to the dresser and laid her down. She could do this. She could change a diaper and get one six-month-old child back to bed without falling apart. After all, you didn't have to become emotionally involved to change a diaper. A couple of minutes and she could crawl back into bed, cuddle up next to Cullen and hope that the warmth of his body would drive away her own inner chill. How long could it take to diaper one baby?

Longer than she'd anticipated. Especially when that baby was more interested in kicking and squirming than in getting a dry diaper. When Darcy started trying to pull off the plastic pants, Angie drew her knees up and waved her arms. A brief but vehement struggle later, Darcy was the proud possessor of both plastic pants and soggy diaper. Angie grinned at her and babbled happily.

"Don't tell me you were trying to help," Darcy muttered.

She dropped the diaper in the diaper pail and pulled a fresh one from the stack nearby. Angie kicked both legs, delighted to find herself bare bottomed, pleased to find herself with an audience at one o'clock in the morning. Or maybe just delighted with life in general.

Darcy smiled despite herself. It must be nice to be six months old and have nothing to worry about except growing up. Not that Angie's life had been picture-book perfect so far. Finding herself an orphan at six months was not exactly part of a fairy tale. But Angie had had Cullen to come to her rescue. Darcy folded a diaper and managed to get it under the baby.

Cullen had come to her rescue, too, though he

probably didn't realize it. Before she'd met him, her
life had been painted in shades of gray. Largely by
her own choice, Darcy admitted to herself. She'd
spent years building fences around herself, making
sure she didn't get too close to anyone, that she didn't
open herself to that kind of hurt.

And then she'd met Cullen and he didn't seem to
notice the fences or, if he did, he'd chosen to cut
through them. And she'd suddenly found herself living in a world of color again. Did he have any idea
what he'd done? Did he know he'd dragged her out
of her shell, made her feel again? Made her vulner-
able again?

"You're a very lucky little girl," she told Angie.
"Your uncle Cullen is a very special man and you're
lucky to have him. *I'm* lucky to have him."

But would she have him much longer?

She pushed the question away as she finished diapering the wiggling baby and picked her up. Despite
the tiredness revealed by her heavy-lidded eyes,
Angie didn't seem to have any immediate plans to go
back to sleep. Darcy couldn't help but smile at the
infant's determination.

"You're a stubborn little thing, aren't you?"

Angie muttered, her eyelids drooping a little before
being forced upward. Darcy rocked her gently, keeping her voice to a singsong rhythm.

"Afraid you'll miss something important if you go
to sleep? It'll all still be there in the morning."

She continued to talk to the baby, nonsensical
words, their meaning less important than the sound of
her voice. As she spoke, she forgot about keeping her

distance, about holding herself aloof. The soft weight in her arms felt sweetly familiar and right.

The dimly lit room was a pleasant haven, safe and secure. Darcy began to sing quietly to the baby, momentarily forgetting all the reasons she couldn't let herself get close to this small scrap of humanity, and allowing herself to simply enjoy the feel of having her arms full again after being empty for so long.

Chapter Three

The man standing in the doorway thought he'd never seen anything more beautiful in his life than the picture the woman and child made. Darcy was wearing a plain white T-shirt, size extralarge, that came halfway down her thighs. Cullen had never understood how something as basic as a T-shirt could look so sexy, but one thing he'd learned in the past six months was that Darcy Logan could probably make a trash bag look sexy.

But it wasn't sex he was thinking of at the moment. Or at least, that wasn't *all* he was thinking of, he amended, looking at the smooth length of leg beneath the hem of the T-shirt. Until this moment he hadn't realized just how beautiful a woman could look holding a baby. The tenderness in Darcy's expression as she looked down at Angie sparked a warmth somewhere deep inside Cullen.

She looked so utterly natural holding the baby, so right. The very picture of mother and child. For a moment he felt a piercing grief at the thought of his sister, who would never again hold her baby and sing to her. But a part of Susan remained behind in little Angie. He couldn't bring his sister back but he could do his best to live up to the faith she'd had in him. He'd raise her child for her. With Darcy's help, he hoped.

She'd been so uncomfortable around the baby that he'd begun to wonder if Darcy was afraid of her. God knew, he could sympathize with the feeling, he thought ruefully. Angie scared the life out of him. There was no reason Darcy wouldn't feel the same.

As far as he knew, she didn't have much experience with babies. Though she'd certainly known enough to guide him through his first fumbling attempts at some of the basics like diapering and bathing and feeding. At the time he'd been too grateful for her knowledge to question its source. Vaguely, he'd thought it must be some inborn instinct that women had, but he doubted that knowing how to put on a diaper was part of the genetic code.

Now here she was holding Angie as easily as if she'd been doing it since the child was born. He envied her that look of easy competence even as he wondered how she'd come by it. It occurred to him that, despite the months they'd lived together, there was a great deal he didn't know about her. The present had been so absorbing that there hadn't seemed to be much reason to discuss past histories. Maybe it was time to think about changing that.

"You're very good with her," Cullen said quietly.

Darcy jumped and turned toward him, careful not to disturb the now-sleeping baby. The light was dim, but for an instant he thought she looked guilty, as if she'd been caught doing something she shouldn't. The guilt—if that's what it had been—disappeared immediately, replaced by the carefully neutral expression he was coming to associate with anything to do with the baby.

"It doesn't take any talent to change a diaper," she said lightly.

"I don't know about that." Cullen's smile was rueful as he came into the room. "It took me quite a few tries to master the skill, and I wouldn't have managed at all if you hadn't shown me how."

"You'd have figured it out. A man who can build a house isn't likely to be permanently stumped by a diaper." Darcy's tone was quiet but matter-of-fact.

"Houses don't wiggle while you're trying to nail up the next stud," he pointed out. "The first time I tried to change her, I'd have been willing to swear she had six legs and all of them moving at once. If you hadn't come to my rescue, I'd still be in that hotel room in Seattle trying to get her to hold still long enough for me to sort everything out."

"If you'd waited for her to hold still, you would still be waiting. Babies don't do still very well." She carried Angie over to the crib and Cullen followed, watching as she eased the infant down onto the mattress.

"So I've learned. Where did you learn so much about babies?" It was a casual question but he felt Darcy stiffen and there was a tiny pause before she answered.

"Baby-sitting," she said. "I did a lot of baby-sitting when I was a teenager."

"I didn't know that."

"No reason you should," she said, lifting one shoulder in a half shrug.

Her tone was so completely normal that Cullen wondered if he'd imagined that brief moment of tension. He reached down to tug a pink cotton blanket up over Angie.

"She'll just kick it off," Darcy pointed out.

"I know." Cullen brushed the back of one finger over Angie's cheek, marveling at the softness of her skin. "She's so small and helpless," he murmured. "It's kind of scary when you think about how dependent she is. Makes you a little nervous, you know."

"I know." Something in her tone brought his head up, but she turned away before he could see her expression. "Since she's settled, I'm going back to bed."

"I'll be in in a minute." But he was speaking to her back.

As Darcy left the room, Cullen turned back to the sleeping baby. Resting his hands on the top rail of the crib, he looked down at her, but for the first time in a week, he wasn't really seeing her. He was seeing Darcy the way she'd looked when he'd first come in, her face soft and practically glowing with tenderness. As soon as she'd realized he was there, that expression had disappeared, wiped from her face as if it had never been. As if there was something wrong with her showing affection toward Angie.

In the short time they'd lived together, he'd learned that Darcy was a very private woman. She reminded him of an iceberg, concealing so much more than she ever revealed. He had the feeling that she kept an important part of herself hidden away from him. Sometimes he wondered if he knew her at all.

Angie shifted in her sleep and the little blanket

slipped halfway off. With a half smile, Cullen tugged it back over her tiny form. Brushing the tip of one finger over her cheek, he turned and left the room.

Darcy was in bed when Cullen entered their bedroom. Her eyes had had time to adjust to the darkness and she watched as he pushed the door partially shut behind him and crossed to the bed. His chest was bare and she let her gaze drift over the mat of dark hair that covered muscles hardened by physical labor. Cullen was as likely to be found swinging a hammer as he was reading blueprints.

Though she couldn't see it in this light, she knew his skin was tanned from working in the sun without a shirt. The hair on his chest tapered to a dark line that arrowed across the flat plane of his stomach before disappearing into the low-slung waist of the black, cotton pajama bottoms he wore.

Despite her emotional turmoil, she felt desire stir in the pit of her stomach. Though they'd slept together every night, they hadn't made love since he'd gotten word about his sister's death, nearly two weeks past.

He stopped beside the bed. There wasn't enough light for her to read his expression but she could see the glitter of his eyes and knew he was looking at her. Perhaps it was the darkness or the lateness of the hour or the stress of the past couple of weeks, but it seemed to Darcy that he was suddenly almost overwhelmingly male.

He seemed to loom over the bed and when he lowered his hands to shove the pajama bottoms off his narrow hips, the hunger that tightened her belly was mixed with a touch of purely feminine uneasiness. She wasn't afraid of him but she was abruptly aware of the very definite differences between a man and a woman. He was so much stronger than she. There was comfort in that knowledge but a part of her acknowledged the potential danger inherent in that strength.

Her breath caught in her throat as the black cotton slid off his hips, revealing the strength of his arousal. Cullen must have heard the revealing sound because he grinned with pure masculine arrogance. If she hadn't been melting inside, Darcy would have been tempted to sock him in the ribs as punishment for that look. The throbbing ache in the pit of her stomach urged her to pull him down to her, to let him soothe that ache as only he could do.

She might have done just that if he hadn't grinned again and set his hands on his hips, bending one knee in a classic masculine pose, flaunting himself with infuriating impudence, daring her to resist him. She couldn't and he knew it, damn his blue eyes. But that didn't mean she had to give in without a fight.

Darcy eased out from under the covers and stood up. Without a glance in Cullen's direction, she grasped the hem of the plain white T-shirt and eased it slowly upward, baring her body an inch at a time.

Cullen felt his mouth go dry as she drew the shirt up over her hips, exposing the triangle of soft blond curls at the top of her thighs. The slender curve of her waist and the inviting hollow of her belly button were next and then she paused. She gave him a sidelong glance that he felt all the way to his toes.

She inched the shirt a little higher, baring her midriff and the beginning swell of her breasts. His fingers curled into his palms as he fought the urge to grab her and rip the shirt from her before tumbling her back onto the bed. She looked at him again, as if measuring his desire. Apparently satisfied with what she saw, she drew the T-shirt the rest of the way off.

Cullen stopped breathing. It didn't matter how many times he saw her like this, he was never prepared for the impact she had on his senses. Her full breasts swayed as she tossed the T-shirt away. She lifted her hands and ran them through her hair, turning slightly so that he had a perfect view of the inviting thrust of her breasts as her arms lifted.

It was a game they'd played before, teasing each other with pretended indifference, driving each other crazy by looking but not touching. The game had only one ending, but there was pleasure in drawing it out, in building the fires slowly, letting the heat climb.

Tonight, Cullen wasn't in the mood to draw things out. It seemed as if it had been months since he'd touched her, forever since he'd touched that smooth, golden skin.

Darcy gasped when his hands closed over her hips, his fingers curving into her soft bottom as he pulled her up against his hard body with almost violent force. She threw her head back, her urgency rising to meet his. His mouth came down on hers, his tongue plunging into her mouth with no preliminaries, only a stark, driving hunger that added to the ache in her.

Her fingers dug into the rock-hard muscles of his upper arms. She twisted herself closer. His arousal was hot and hard against the softness of her belly, making her whimper with hunger. It seemed as if it had been so long since he'd held her like this, loved her like this.

Cullen lowered her to the bed, bracing his arm against the mattress as he followed her down. His knee slid between hers, and Darcy opened her legs to him, the tension inside coiling almost painfully tight.

"I don't want to wait." His voice was husky as the tip of his erection brushed against the dampness of her most sensitive flesh.

"Who asked you to?" she got out breathlessly. The arch of her hips was an irresistible invitation.

Cullen's first thrust took him deep within her, filling the emptiness. Darcy sucked in her breath and arched her body to take him deeper still. She needed to feel him all the way to her soul, needed to know that he was hers and hers alone.

Cullen groaned as he felt the heated dampness of her surround him. He felt completed, made whole in a way only she could do. He caught her hands in his, pinning them flat to the bed as he withdrew and thrust again.

Darcy dug her heels into the bed and arched to meet him. He lowered his body to hers, the muscular width of his chest crushing her breasts, the crisp mat of hair abrading her tender nipples. There was a tightly coiled spring low inside her belly and every thrust, every brush of his body against hers drew the coils tighter still until it seemed as if the pressure of it was more than she could bear.

And then Cullen's hands slid under her, his fingers

digging into the soft flesh of her bottom, pulling her up to meet his solid penetration of her, deepening an embrace that couldn't possibly get any deeper, making her his all the way to her soul.

And the tension inside her shattered into tiny fragments of sensation. If she'd had the breath to do so, Darcy might have screamed. But he'd stolen her breath, her soul, her heart. She dug her fingers into the damp muscles of his shoulders, sobbing with the force of her pleasure.

Cullen groaned as he felt her climax take her. She shuddered beneath him as tiny muscles rippled and contracted around him, dragging him headlong into his own satisfaction. He pulled her higher on his invading flesh, feeling Darcy's nails bite into his shoulders as the movement prolonged her own pleasure.

And then he gave himself up and let the heavy pulse of release take him.

Through eyes blurred with tears of pleasure, Darcy saw Cullen's face above her, the skin tight across his cheekbones, his lips drawn back from his teeth, a guttural groan bursting from him. She lifted her legs and locked her ankles across his lower back, arching her body into his. He shuddered against her as the movement deepened their already impossibly deep embrace. The pleasure seemed to go on and on, long rolling waves of sensation.

It was a long time before Darcy gathered the strength to open her eyes. She felt heavy with exhaustion yet so light that it seemed possible she might float up from the bed without Cullen's weight to hold her down. There was a pleasant tingly feeling to her skin.

Cullen shifted, easing his weight onto his elbows and looking down at her. It was too dark for her to read his expression but she caught the white gleam of his teeth as he smiled.

"That'll teach you to tease, Ms. Logan."

"I've certainly learned my lesson, Mr. Roberts." Her voice was almost as steady as his.

"See that you don't forget." The last word ended on a groan as she tightened certain muscles, demonstrating an admirable grasp of the situation.

"I certainly wouldn't want to tease," she said, widening her eyes in a show of innocence at odds with the far from innocent movement of her body.

"I can see that you wouldn't." Cullen flexed his hips, letting her feel his growing arousal.

"I wouldn't want to disturb you." It took considerable effort to keep her voice steady.

"I like being disturbed." Cullen wrapped his hands in her hair, using the hold to tilt her head back. Darcy shivered as she felt his teeth against the taut line of her throat.

It wasn't as urgent this time. Arousal built slowly, drugging her senses, melting her body into his until it was hard to tell where one stopped and the other began. Her response to Cullen never failed to surprise her. She'd always thought of herself as a rather cold person. But Cullen brought out a fire in her that sometimes threatened to consume her.

She moaned, her fingers clinging to his shoulders as the world rocked around them once more.

And for a little while Darcy could push aside her fears that she was going to lose him.

Chapter Four

"I can't believe that one baby requires all this stuff just to go out to dinner. A small army could march across the Gobi with less."

Darcy grinned as she watched Cullen struggle with the car seat and a bulging diaper bag. It was the first time they'd ventured out of the house with Angie in the two weeks since they'd picked her up in Seattle.

"An army doesn't have to cater to the needs of a baby," she told him.

"Well, if this is what it takes, there'd be a lot fewer wars if they did. Three months in boot camp couldn't prepare a man for carting all this stuff around," he groused. "Not to mention they'd be too tired to fight because they'd never manage to get a decent night's sleep."

The last was a mutter as he walked out the door to put his burdens in the car. Darcy was left alone with the baby. She looked at Angie, who was lying on the sofa with pillows mounded around her to keep her from rolling off. Having pulled one sock off, Angie was doing her best to bite her toes.

Darcy's hands twitched with the urge to pick her up but she resisted. She'd had plenty of time to think about the situation. Since coming back from Seattle, she'd thought of little else. The situation seemed impossible: she wanted nothing to do with having a baby in her life but Cullen now came with a baby attached.

And the one thing she was absolutely sure of was that she *did* want Cullen in her life. The realization of just how much was rather frightening to someone who'd spent the past six years carefully wanting nothing and most especially wanting no one. She'd lived with Cullen almost six months, but it had taken Angie's arrival to make her realize how much she'd come to depend on him, how much she needed him.

Her first reaction to the baby had been denial. If she told herself he didn't matter so much, then he wouldn't. But she'd never been much good at lying to herself. The truth was that she couldn't bear the thought of going back to the sterile, empty, *safe* existence she'd led before Cullen had come into her life. The happiness she'd found with him might be fragile—he'd surely hate her if he ever learned the full truth about her. But fragile or not, she didn't want to give it up, didn't want to give up the man who'd given it to her.

And since she couldn't ask Cullen to give up his sister's child, she was going to have to find a way to come to terms with Angie's presence in her life. Not so complex really, she told herself as she watched the baby contentedly playing with her own toes. Cullen hadn't noticed anything odd about her behavior toward his niece so far. And if he did, she'd just tell him she wasn't the maternal type. Then all she had to do was keep a little emotional and physical distance between herself and Angie.

How hard could that be?

Losing interest in her toes, Angie looked around for a new distraction. Her flailing hand found the stuffed cloth block she'd been playing with before discovering the delights of toe chewing. She lifted it and studied it with a seriousness worthy of an entomologist examining a new species of beetle. Her eyes were exactly the color of her uncle's, that same clear, heart-melting blue. Darcy found herself smiling at Angie's serious expression.

"Ready?" Cullen's question preceded him. Darcy's head jerked toward the door as he entered.

"Yes." *There was nothing to feel guilty about,* she scolded herself.

"How are my two best girls?" At the sound of Cullen's voice, Angie abruptly lost interest in the block. Her head turned until she found him. Immediately her small face creased into a two-toothed grin and she began to kick both her feet in excitement.

Cullen's answering grin was nothing short of enthralled, Darcy thought as she watched him walk over to the sofa. Despite the lack of sleep he'd complained about, he looked devastatingly handsome. A shock of dark hair fell onto his forehead, emphasizing the blue of his eyes. He was wearing black jeans and a blue shirt almost the exact shade of his eyes. She'd bought him that shirt for Christmas. Now she almost wished she hadn't. He didn't need anything to make him look more attractive. The man practically qualified as a lethal weapon as it was.

"How's my girl?" he asked Angie as he leaned down to pick her up. His hands looked huge against her small body but he held her easily, with none of the uncertainty he'd shown at first. Held in midair, Angie babbled happily, both legs churning with the excitement of having Cullen's attention.

I know just how you feel, Darcy thought wryly.

The restaurant was new to both of them, a family kind of place with a menu that ran more toward hot roast beef sandwiches with mashed potatoes than filet mignon with tiny vegetables.

"I didn't think Angie was ready for Chez Bev," Cullen said, mentioning a restaurant they'd been to several times.

"I doubt they're ready for her, either." Darcy's tone was dry, but she didn't look particularly disappointed by his choice of restaurants, Cullen thought, glancing at her as he settled Angie into a high chair.

"You could be right. Imagine the waiter's expression if she spit a mouthful of baby carrots at him." He latched the tray in place before sliding into the red vinyl booth.

"It would cause a major crisis," Darcy agreed. "The chef would probably come out to ask her what it was about his special recipe that didn't appeal to her."

"I'm not sure her French is up to task," Cullen said seriously.

Angie babbled something and slapped both hands against the metal tray of the high chair as if demanding to know where dinner was.

"I don't know. I think she could get her message across in most languages," Darcy said dryly.

"You could be right." Cullen found a toy in the

bulging diaper bag and handed it to his niece to distract her from the delay with mealtime. Angie promptly began to gnaw on the plastic ring.

Seeing that she was occupied, at least momentarily, he turned his attention to Darcy. One thing he'd learned about babies was the truly amazing amount of time they required. It seemed as if he hadn't had time to draw a breath. He'd been telling himself that he and Darcy would talk, that they'd discuss the changes Angie had made in their lives. But it had been two weeks and they'd yet to talk.

He'd never realized just how big a job it was to take care of a baby, especially since he'd been thrown in at the deep end without the slightest preparation for the task. Without his secretary, who'd been willing to extend her job description to include shopping, and Darcy to show him the fine points of diapering, among other things, he doubted if either he or Angie would have made it to the end of the first week.

He thought he was starting to get the hang of it now, but it still seemed as if most of his waking hours were spent dealing with the minutiae of life with a baby. And the brief bits of time he had for anything else were spent trying to keep up with his business. Kiel hadn't complained about dealing with his partner's work as well as his own but Cullen didn't expect him to keep doing it. Besides, there were decisions that took the two of them to make. Add Darcy's job to the mix and the end result was that the two of them hadn't had a moment to themselves.

Except in bed. They communicated just fine there. But when he was in bed with Darcy, his urges ran to something more elemental than discussing life changes.

But now, here they were, alone, unless you counted Angie and the couple of hundred other patrons in the restaurant. It wasn't exactly intimate and he hadn't planned on starting a serious discussion tonight but maybe they could talk without too many interruptions.

"Darcy, I—"

"What can I get for you?" Their waitress looked about eighteen. She wore the same nondescript brown and white uniform the other waitresses wore but she'd accessorized hers with black ankle socks, combat boots and a small gold stud through one nostril.

Cullen managed to keep his expression under control until the girl had taken their order and left. Once she was gone, he leaned across the table.

"Who do you think does her makeup?" he asked, keeping his voice low.

"Lon Chaney. I'm sure I saw that same look in the original *Phantom of the Opera*. It's the hair I'm not sure about."

"You mean that spiky thing on top of her head is her hair?" Cullen widened his eyes in mock disbelief. "How does she get it to stand up like that?"

"Years of practice and a can of mousse."

The girl returned with their drinks. Once she was gone, Cullen's eyes met Darcy's and she dissolved in giggles. His rich chuckle joined her laughter. Angie chortled happily, unconcerned with the cause of the adults' good humor.

"We haven't laughed much lately, have we?" he said as their laughter faded.

"Things have been a little hectic." Darcy reached for the pottery cream pitcher and added a generous dollop to her coffee.

"That's an understatement." Angie threw the purple plastic ring onto the table and Cullen automatically returned it to her.

"I'm a banker. We're supposed to understate things." Darcy reached for her spoon. The plastic ring landed right next it and Darcy picked it up and set it on the high chair's tray.

"I know I said we'd talk—about the baby and everything. We need—" This time Angie threw the ring on the floor and then leaned over to look at the results of her effort. Cullen bent and scooped it up and started to hand it to her.

"She'll put it in her mouth," Darcy commented.

"What?" His thoughts on other things, he stared at her blankly.

"She'll put that in her mouth." Darcy nodded to the ring. "It's been on the floor."

"Oh. Right." He turned and stuffed the ring back into the diaper bag and came up with a cloth ball. Angie took it from him with a squeal of delight.

"Not that it really matters."

"Not that what matters?" he asked, feeling as if he'd lost the thread of the conversation.

"Whether or not she put that in her mouth after it had been on the floor. If she can survive chewing on her own feet, I suspect she's tough enough to survive the little bit of dirt it might have picked up."

"Then why did you stop me from giving it to her?"

"Because there's a grandmotherly looking type at the counter who's keeping an eye on us, and I was afraid she'd slap your hand if you did something she disapproved of."

Cullen looked in the direction she'd indicated, his glance colliding with that of an older woman who was sitting at the lunch counter. She beamed at him. He smiled in return and then turned back to Darcy, who was watching him over the rim of her coffee cup, her gray eyes bright with humor.

"Why is she looking at me like that?" he asked sotto voce, as if the woman might actually be able to hear him from fifteen feet away.

"She's impressed by how good you are with the baby."

"I haven't done anything." He returned the cloth ball to Angie, who'd flung it into the middle of the table. She promptly threw it again. Fetch was one of her favorite games, as long as someone else was doing the fetching.

His patience with Angie was so effortless that he wasn't even aware of it, Darcy thought. He'd turned his entire life upside down without a second thought to give his niece a home. And he didn't even see anything extraordinary about what he'd done. Watching him with the baby, it occurred to her that he was born to be a father. The role fit him like a well-tailored suit.

The realization seemed to open a gaping chasm between them, with her on one side and Cullen and the baby on the other. The bright lights suddenly seemed a little blurred and there was a constriction in her throat. She lowered her head and pretended to search for something in her purse while she got her emotions under control.

"Are you all right?"

Cullen leaned across the table and Darcy didn't have to look at him to know that he was looking concerned. Why couldn't he do things the way men were traditionally supposed to do them? Why couldn't he be an insensitive lout, oblivious to her feelings?

"I'm fine," she said, dragging a crumpled tissue from the bottom of her purse and dabbing it against one eye. "I just had something in my eye. It's out now."

She lifted her head and gave him a bright smile to show that everything was peachy keen. Cullen looked doubtful and she had the feeling that he might have pursued the issue if the waitress hadn't chosen that moment to return with their order.

"Here you go."

If Darcy had been starving to death, she couldn't have been any more grateful to see a waitress. Spiky hair, nose stud, combat boots and all, the girl couldn't have looked better if she'd been wearing white wings.

"Here's our food," she said cheerfully, just in case Cullen hadn't noticed the plates being set in front of them. She knew, even if Cullen hadn't yet figured it out, that there wasn't much chance of having an intelligent conversation while feeding a six-month-old baby.

He might want to talk about the changes in their situation, but she didn't. She didn't want to have to try to find a way to tell him that she'd continue to live with him but that she wanted to have as little as possible to do with the baby. He was sure to want to know why and she didn't have the words to give him. Unless she told him the truth and that was out of the question.

Apparently, Cullen realized that serious conversation and feeding a baby were not compatible activities. Darcy gradually relaxed as the conversation stayed on relatively neutral ground. She told him what had been going on at her job. He mentioned a new construction project that he and Kiel were going to bid on.

It was so much the kind of conversation they'd always had that if she closed her eyes, Darcy could almost have believed that it was B.B.—Before Baby.

She watched with admiration as he managed to eat his meal while feeding Angie. She'd never been half so good with— She cut the thought off, turning her thoughts from that particular path. It wasn't difficult, she'd had years of practice.

They were nearly finished with their dinner when the older woman who'd smiled at Cullen earlier approached the table.

"I hope you don't mind, but I just had to get a closer look at your baby."

"Not at all," Cullen said, casting a quick look in Darcy's direction. She shrugged. He'd learn that babies had a way of starting conversations between total strangers, whether you wished it or not.

"I couldn't help but notice her when you brought her in." She leaned over to peer at Angie, who gave her a cheerful smile. "Not a shy bone in her body," the woman said delightedly. "She's the spitting image of my Wanda. Not now, of course, because she turned forty-eight this last March. She says she's only forty-one but that's not something a mother's likely to forget, now is it?"

She fixed Darcy with bright blue eyes and Darcy nodded obediently. "I can't imagine how."

"Exactly what I told Wanda. Besides, I have her birth certificate," Wanda's mother said triumphantly.

"I doubt these folks want to hear about that, Millie." Millie's husband had been standing behind her, looking mildly embarrassed by his wife's chatter.

"I suppose not, but it's just so exasperating. I mean, she can have all the nips and tucks she wants and dress up like a teenager and I don't say a word about it, but it seems to me she's going a bit far when she starts lying to her own mother about her age."

Silence seemed the only safe response. Darcy saw a suspicious tuck in Cullen's cheek and knew he was struggling to hold back a laugh. Obviously he was in no hurry to leap into the conversation.

"Millie." Mr. Millie was starting to look as if he wished he were somewhere else.

"All right. I'll stop nattering on." Millie smiled down at Angie again. "I just had to tell you two what a beautiful little girl you have here. Not that I can't see that you already know that," she added. "She's lucky to have parents who care for her the way you two obviously do."

"Oh, but—"

"Thank you." Cullen's voice cut across Darcy's

automatic attempt to correct the woman's assumption that they were Angie's parents.

With a last smile at the baby, Millie departed. At another time Darcy would have been amused to see that Mr. Millie had his hand firmly around his wife's upper arm as if to prevent her from dashing back to talk some more.

But there was a funny ache in her chest that made it difficult to see the humor in the scene. It was silly to let something so small cause her pain. What did it matter that Millie-Wanda's mother thought Angie was her child?

It didn't matter at all except that, for a moment, she'd have given almost anything for it to be true.

"I didn't see any reason to get into explanations," Cullen said.

"No, of course not." Darcy forced a smile as she looked at him. "She was quite a character, wasn't she?"

"I think her husband was about ready to gag her."

"I have a sneaking sympathy with poor Wanda." Darcy wondered if it was her imagination that made Cullen's humor seem a little forced. "All that nipping and tucking and then betrayed by your own mother."

"Must be rough."

They finished their meal, though Darcy could barely remember what she was eating. She refused dessert with a smile. The tightness in her stomach made her wonder if she'd be able to keep down what she'd already eaten.

Angie was asleep almost as soon as Cullen strapped her into her car seat. The drive home was silent, with

Darcy pretending an intense interest in the scene out-side her window. She knew, with an instinct she didn't question, that Cullen had every intention of having that long-delayed talk tonight. The one that would inevitably involve some discussion of the fu-ture, of Darcy's place in the future he and Angie were bound to share.

Logically, she supposed such a discussion couldn't be postponed forever, not when it involved Angie's future. But surely it could be delayed just one more night.

Cullen turned the car into the slot in front of the condo and it had barely stopped moving before she reached for the door handle.

"I'll get the diaper bag," she said, snatching it up and making her escape.

It took time to get a baby out of a car seat. Maybe she could be in the shower by the time Cullen reached the condo. She might have succeeded in doing just that if it hadn't taken even more time than usual to dig her keys out of the bottom of her cavernous purse. She was going to get a smaller purse, she promised herself as Cullen joined her on the porch, the baby asleep in his arms. Or a bigger key chain.

"I'm going to hop in the shower," she said without looking at him.

"Darcy." Cullen's voice halted her flight across the living room. "I'd like to talk to you."

"Could it wait?" she asked without turning.

"I think it's waited long enough."

"I was just—"

"Please."

The single word was more effective than if he'd shouted. She stopped and turned to look at him, trying to keep the uneasiness from her voice.

"It's getting late—"

"It's not even nine o'clock."

"I have to get up in the morning."

"It's Saturday. You can sleep in."

He wasn't going to give up. Darcy sighed.

"Why don't you put Angie to bed?" She ran her fingers through her hair, letting it tumble back to her shoulders like a pale gold curtain. "I'll put some coffee on."

"Thanks." They both knew he wasn't thanking her for making coffee.

Chapter Five

Cullen stopped in the kitchen doorway and indulged himself by simply looking at Darcy. The warm scent of coffee filled the air. She was getting mugs from the cupboard. Their position on the second shelf meant she had to reach to get them and her T-shirt rode up, baring a swatch of pale skin above the waist of her jeans.

He knew the taste of that skin, knew that if he dragged his tongue along the length of her spine, she'd tremble with need. He knew the way the soft flesh of her bottom yielded beneath his fingers. Knew that kissing the back of her knee made her giggle. He knew every inch of her, every muscle, every nerve, just where to touch her to have her dissolve in his arms.

She was his. He hadn't been her first lover but he'd been the first to satisfy her, the first to show her the potential of her own body. He'd never asked about her past lovers, any more than she'd asked about his. Never questioned her shocked surprise the first time she'd come apart in his bed.

Whoever the man was—and he had the feeling there'd only been one—he'd been a fool. But Cullen admitted to a sneaking feeling of gratitude toward the unknown fool. He liked it that he'd been the one to introduce Darcy to passion. He didn't care if he was first but he damn well wanted to be last.

As if sensing his gaze, Darcy turned suddenly to face him, her fingers tight around the cups she held.

"I didn't hear you," she said, her voice a little sharp with surprise.

"Sorry. I'll try to learn to stomp." Cullen pushed himself away from the door and came farther into the kitchen. "Coffee smells good. Thanks for making it."

"You're welcome. It's decaf. I didn't think either one of us needed caffeine at this time of night."

"You're probably right." He certainly didn't need anything to keep him awake and she looked tense enough to shatter at any moment.

She set the mugs on the counter and poured coffee in them while Cullen got a carton of half-and-half from the refrigerator.

"Did you get Angie to bed all right?"

"Out like a light."

Cullen poured a dollop of half-and-half into the mug decorated with a lavender and white carousel horse. The other mug displayed a folk-art-style painting of a cat. The mugs were among Darcy's contributions to their living arrangements. Before she'd moved in with him, he'd had two plates, two forks, two knives, two of everything. And the only coffee cup he'd owned had been a chipped white cup that looked as if it had been recovered from the wreck of the *Titanic*. Darcy's collection of colorful mugs was only one of the many ways she'd brightened his life.

Without discussing it, they took their coffee into the living room. Darcy curled up on the sofa. Cullen chose the big leather chair that sat at an angle nearby. He took a sip of his coffee and then stared down into it. Darcy took a sip of hers and then studied a piece of lint on the arm of the sofa.

The silence was deafening.

"I wanted—"

"You said—"

They both broke off and looked at each other. Cullen nodded. "You first."

"I was just going to mention that you'd said you wanted to talk to me."

"Funny. I was just going to mention the same thing." His smile was rueful. Darcy's was uncertain. But the tension that had been threatening to suffocate both of them was broken.

Cullen set his cup down on the thick sheet of glass that formed the top of the coffee table. It was supported by a gnarled piece of driftwood. He was going to have to get a new coffee table, he thought absently, noting the sharp corners of glass. Either that or find a way to pad the edges of this one. Angie was already standing up with a bit of support. According to what he'd read, it wouldn't be long until she was trying to walk and he didn't want her to crack her head open on the coffee table.

He said as much. Darcy looked surprised but she glanced at the table and nodded.

"The edges could probably be padded, maybe tape some old towels to the glass." She shook her head, her mouth curving in a half smile. "Early American Baby decor."

"Not likely to start any new trends."

"Well, it might not attract the designer crowd," she agreed.

"Do you mind?" he asked abruptly.

"That *House & Garden* isn't beating a path to our door?" She raised her brows.

"That there've been so many…changes because of the baby." He saw her fingers tighten around the mug and her eyes shifted away from his.

"I think it goes with the territory," she said lightly.

"Yes. But I couldn't blame you if you resented it." He set down his barely touched coffee and stood up. There was too much churning inside him for him to sit still. "You didn't ask for any of this."

"You didn't, either."

"No. But Susan was *my* sister, not yours." He turned and paced to the sliding-glass door that led out onto the patio. Twitching aside the curtain, he stared out into the darkness, half wishing he hadn't brought the subject up. They'd been rubbing along together all right. Why rock the boat?

Because you don't want it capsizing under you when you least expect it. Because you don't want to lose the best damn thing that's ever happened to you.

He turned back to her with an abruptness that made Darcy jump. "Look, I know I didn't give you any choice about this. And I know I should have. I had no right to throw your life into turmoil without even discussing it with you."

"What was there to discuss?" She leaned forward to set her cup down, the faint tremor in her hand belying the calm reason of her voice. "You couldn't leave Angie where she was and there was no one else who could take her.''

''Yes.'' They were the same arguments he'd used on himself and the logic of them sounded just as inescapable as it had then. But that didn't soothe his conscience. ''I should have—''

''You did exactly what you should have,'' Darcy interrupted. She stood up and walked over to where he stood, setting one slim hand on his arm and looking up at him. ''I'm not upset or angry that you didn't discuss this with me, Cullen. The decision was only yours to make and you couldn't have made any other.''

He stared down at her, an uncharacteristic brooding look in his blue eyes. She was so good at hiding what she was thinking, what she was feeling. It could have been a natural part of her makeup but he'd always suspected that it was something she'd learned through hard experience.

From the first moment he'd met her, he'd seen the shadows in her eyes. Someone or something had hurt her in the past. Hurt her badly enough to put those shadows there. They'd begun to fade over the past few months, as if she were—very slowly—starting to forget whatever it was that had marked her. Or if not forgetting, then at least putting it behind her.

But just lately the shadows were back, turning her clear gray eyes smoky, muting the sparkle he'd come to love. He was afraid she was slipping away from him and if he lost her, he'd lose the best part of his life.

''You're not happy.''

The flat statement hit Darcy with the force of a blow. She let her hand drop from his arm as she took a quick step back, grateful that the light from the single lamp wouldn't be enough to reveal the way the color had drained from her cheeks.

"I don't know what you mean." It was a weak response, but it was the best she could do. She'd been so sure that she'd concealed her feelings from him, so careful not to allow even the smallest crack in the facade.

"I mean, you're...uncomfortable around Angie." Cullen hesitated over the choice of words. The feeling he got from Darcy wasn't discomfort. It was more like fear, but that sounded too ridiculous to say out loud.

"I haven't spent a lot of time around babies, that's all."

"You said you'd done some baby-sitting," he reminded her.

"Baby-sitting is a little different from having one around full time," she said lightly.

"True."

But he continued to look at her, those clear blue eyes asking questions she couldn't—wouldn't—answer. If he knew the real reason...

"I—I guess I'm not really the maternal type," Darcy said, lifting one shoulder in a half shrug. "I mean, I think Angie's adorable and all that, but she doesn't *do* a whole lot, if you know what I mean. You can't talk to her or anything."

She shrugged again, keeping her face turned from the light to hide the color burning in her cheeks. She hadn't realized she had it in her to sound so completely shallow and inane. *You can't talk to her.* As if she expected to be able to discuss Dostoyevski with a six-month-old baby. If Cullen hadn't despised her before, he probably would now.

"I guess that sounds pretty stupid," she muttered when he didn't say anything.

"No. I think I understand what you're saying." What he didn't understand was why she was telling him such a barefaced lie. He didn't doubt that there were a good many people who felt that way. He could even understand it to a certain extent. But he'd have bet any amount of money that that wasn't how Darcy felt.

"I used to think I wanted to be a mother," Darcy said, almost choking on the words. "But I guess maybe I don't have the requisite genes. I know that's not what you want to hear. Obviously you'd like me to say that I'll be a terrific mother to Angie, but I don't think I'm cut out for the job. I know that's a real problem."

She stopped and swallowed hard. It required every bit of self-control to keep her voice level while she said what had to be said. "If you want me to move out—"

"No!" Cullen's response was reassuringly quick and emphatic. "That's the last thing I want."

He reached out and caught her hand in his as if afraid she might dash out the door that instant. Darcy drew a deep breath and closed her eyes for a moment, relief so powerful inside her that her knees actually felt weak.

"I don't want you to go," Cullen said firmly. He pulled her into his arms and Darcy went willingly, resting her head against his chest and feeling the strong beat of his heart beneath her cheek.

"I don't want to go," she said, and Cullen knew the admission didn't come easily.

She guarded herself so carefully, he thought, bending to rest his cheek against the top of her head, inhaling the soft scents of shampoo and soap. Darcy rarely wore perfume and he'd decided that the natural smell of a woman was far more erotic than the most expensive perfume could ever be.

"We'll work things out," he told her.

"But Angie has to come first. I wouldn't want to hurt her."

"We'll work everything out. If the fact that you can't talk to her really bothers you, just wait a year or so. According to Sara Randall, she'll be talking like a magpie by then."

Darcy's laugh was choked and she closed her eyes to hold back tears. What had she ever done to deserve a man like Cullen Roberts? But there was something to what he said. If she could hold on until Angie was a little older, until she wasn't quite so afraid of—

She blocked the thought, focusing instead on the feel of Cullen's arms around her. She always felt safe when he held her.

"We'll work everything out," he said again.

If she'd just tell him what was really bothering her, maybe he'd be able to do something about it, Cullen thought. He felt as if he was shadowboxing. He could get glimpses of the enemy but there was nothing to catch hold of, nothing to tell him what he was fighting.

But he wasn't giving up. He was going to find out what was behind those shadows in Darcy's eyes and he was going to banish them forever.

Cullen rearranged his work schedule, bringing most of his paperwork home with him so that he could take care of Angie. When he had to be out on a site, he left her with Sara Randall's youngest daughter. Divorced, with two children of her own, Marie welcomed the extra money and Cullen knew Angie would be well cared for.

Though it had been less than a month, it was already impossible for him to imagine his life without Angie in it. Until his sister's death, he hadn't given much thought to fatherhood. He'd had a vague idea in the back of his head that he might like to have a child someday but, at thirty-four, he hadn't felt that there was any rush to make plans.

Now, abruptly, he found himself plunged into the deep end of parenthood and enjoying it more than he'd ever have imagined. Every day was a new discovery, for himself as well as for Angie. She'd filled a gap in his life he hadn't even realized was there.

With her and Darcy, his life was complete. All he had to do was figure out a way to prove to Darcy how right the three of them were together.

Darcy had mixed feelings about seeing the ties grow ever stronger between Cullen and his niece. She couldn't wish anything less for either of them, but with each day that passed, it seemed clearer that she didn't—couldn't—fit into the tidy picture before her.

Still, things were better than they had been. Talking with Cullen had helped. She hadn't told him the truth—at least not all of it—but she'd made it clear that he'd better not count on her to round out the happy family picture. And it seemed as if he'd accepted that. He certainly didn't thrust Angie into her arms in an attempt to encourage some kind of bonding between them.

Without the pressure of expectations—even if they had been strictly her own—Darcy found herself, paradoxically, more comfortable around the baby than she had been. She relaxed enough to allow herself to enjoy the innocent pleasure Angie took in everything that happened into her field of vision.

She'd almost forgotten the sheer fun to be had in watching those moments of discovery that came so often for an infant. Angie was fascinated by everything she saw and innocently confident that the world was her personal oyster.

It would have taken a much harder heart than Darcy's not to be touched by the baby's pleasure in life. There was a certain pain in watching Angie, but it wasn't as sharp as she'd expected it to be. Apparently, time really did, if not heal, then at least numb all pain.

As long as Cullen didn't expect her to be responsible for Angie, she could almost let herself believe that things might work out, after all.

The early-summer days slipped by in a not unpleasant pattern. An evening in early June found Darcy and Cullen both at home. Darcy had fixed dinner and afterward they'd settled in the living room. Cullen was reading a list of recent changes in the building code that could affect projects he and Kiel had coming up. Darcy had a new mystery open in her lap, but her attention kept wandering from the book.

After twenty minutes on the same page, with not a word of it sticking in her head, she gave up. She looked up, wondering if Cullen's building codes were as boring as her novel. If they were, maybe he'd be interested in watching an old movie on cable. He was sound asleep, which answered her question about how boring the building codes were, she supposed.

Darcy's features softened as she looked at him. He probably needed the sleep. Between running J&R Construction and taking care of Angie, he was handling two full-time jobs. It was no wonder he was dozing off at seven o'clock.

She caught a movement out the corner of her eye and turned to see Angie crawling in her direction. Well, ''crawl'' wasn't an entirely accurate description. It was more a series of belly flops, but what she lacked in coordination, Angie made up for in determination. Since discovering this new method of locomotion a few days before, she'd become an indefatigable explorer, which had required some hasty redecorating to get every possible danger out of her reach.

Now Angie was making her way toward Darcy with solemn perseverance, her blue eyes fixed on Darcy's bright purple socks. Smiling, Darcy wiggled her toes a little. With a grunt of effort, Angie heaved herself the last few inches and flopped onto her belly in front of her goal. Her tiny fingers closed over Darcy's toes, her grip surprisingly strong.

Darcy wiggled her toes again, enjoying the little girl's intent frown as she studied this new toy. Having examined with sight and touch, there was only one choice left, which was taste.

"Hey." Darcy laughed softly as she leaned forward to scoop the baby up. "It's one thing to chew on your own toes but you can't go around munching on other people's. It's just not done in polite society."

Angie was willing to give up the purple sock in exchange for being held. Besides, her new position put her in reach of other interesting objects. Chubby fingers closed around the gold chain Darcy wore around her neck. The chain had been a birthday gift from Cullen not long after she'd moved in with him and she rarely took it off.

"That was a present from your uncle," she told the baby. Angie didn't lift her eyes but continued to study the chain very seriously. After a moment she leaned forward to taste it. Laughing, Darcy pulled her back. "You're going to have to get over this tendency to put everything in your mouth, punkin."

Deprived of the chain, Angie reached for Darcy's nose. Darcy shook her head free and caught one little hand in hers. Bringing it to her mouth, she nibbled on the tiny fingers, drawing a rich baby chuckle. For a few moments she completely forgot all the reasons she needed to keep her distance, for Angie's sake as well as her own, and she let herself simply enjoy the small person in her arms.

From his position on the sofa, Cullen watched the two of them through slitted eyes. He knew that the instant Darcy realized he was awake, she'd get that oddly guilty look on her face and hand the baby to him.

No maternal feelings, his Aunt Fanny. In the rare moments like this, when she forgot whatever it was that haunted her, she was as natural a mother as it was possible to imagine. Her quiet laughter mixed with Angie's fat chuckles and he thought he'd never heard a sweeter sound in his life.

She loved Angie, whether she knew it or not. And though she'd never said the words, he knew Darcy loved him. And God knew, he loved her more than he'd ever dreamed possible. He'd cajoled her into moving in with him, then he'd waited for her to open her eyes and see that what they had was too special to give up. His becoming Angie's guardian had thrown a monkey wrench in the works, but only for a little while. Surely Darcy was starting to see that they could work things out.

Smiling, she buried her nose in Angie's neck, eliciting squeals of delighted laughter as Angie's chubby hands caught fistfuls of Darcy's pale gold hair. Cullen felt his heart swell with love for them both and he was unashamed of the sharp sting of tears at the backs of his eyes.

He was willing to admit to a few doubts, but now he knew that it was going to be all right, after all.

Chapter Six

"What have you got planned for today?" Cullen asked. He was sitting at the table, feeding Angie her breakfast when Darcy walked into the kitchen.

"Shopping. And I wanted to catch up on some paperwork I brought home with me yesterday. Everyone and their dog wants a loan. There aren't enough hours in the day to get everything done."

She opened the refrigerator and peered inside, hoping for inspiration. The sight of last night's leftover pizza made her stomach churn sluggishly and she shut the door. Maybe she'd just have a cup of coffee this morning.

She'd awakened in the middle of the night again last night and had been unable to resist the need to go into the nursery and stand next to the crib, watching the steady rise and fall of the baby's breathing. Reassured, she'd gone back to bed, only to wake an hour later, trembling in the aftermath of a nightmare. It was the third night this week that her sleep had been chopped up and the strain was starting to tell. She felt gray and worn.

"You look tired," Cullen commented as she poured herself a cup of coffee and sat down across the table from him.

"Thanks," she said dryly. "Nice to know I'm looking my best."

"I didn't say you looked bad. I said you looked tired." He fed the baby a spoonful of carrots, deftly scraping the excess off her chin.

"There's a difference?" She took a sip of coffee, hoping the caffeine would jump start her sluggish brain.

"I heard you get up last night."

"I had a little trouble sleeping. Too much going on at work, I guess." She shrugged. To her relief, Cullen accepted the explanation for her insomnia without question.

"You need a day off."

"This *is* my day off."

"Not if you've brought home paperwork." He managed to sneak another bite of carrots into Angie's mouth. She pursed her lips as if to spit them out, saw Cullen watching her and grinned instead. He shuddered.

"You have disgusting table manners," he told her firmly. She banged her spoon on the metal tray of her high chair and squealed her delight at this description.

"I don't think she believes you," Darcy commented.

Hearing her voice, Angie turned and favored Darcy with the same carrot-smeared grin. Darcy smiled back, feeling that odd little twist in her chest that had become so familiar in the weeks since Angie had come to live with them. She was such a beautiful little girl. It would be so easy to love her. If only she dared take that risk.

"Can your paperwork wait?"

Cullen's question drew her attention back to him.

He'd dampened a cloth and was busy wiping carrot off of Angie's face and hands.

"I suppose it could. Why?"

"Because we're going on a picnic."

"A picnic?"

"You know, one of those meals where you sit on the cold, hard ground, fending off wasps and ants and getting sunburned. A picnic."

She wrinkled her nose at him. "You make it sound so appealing."

"The challenge is half the fun," he said briskly. He stood up and lifted Angie out of her high chair. She kicked madly. "I've arranged for Marie to take Angie for the day."

Darcy hesitated over the refusal she'd been about to give him. "Just the two of us?"

"I thought it might be nice for a change."

"I don't mind if Angie comes along," she said quickly. "She's a good baby."

"She's a pest." Since he was tickling Angie's toes at the time, it was clear that "pest" was not the pejorative it might have been. Settling the baby in one arm, he looked at Darcy, his azure eyes holding an expression that made Darcy's heart beat a little faster.

"I want some time without distractions. And being a distraction ranks high on Angie's best talents."

"I really should do some of that paperwork," she said slowly.

"The paperwork won't go anywhere. Come on, Darcy. Play hooky with me."

The coaxing tone was more than she could resist, as was the thought of having him to herself for a

whole afternoon. She didn't resent Angie's demands
on his time but she wouldn't have been human if she
didn't miss the times when it had been just the two
of them.

"Okay. A picnic sounds like fun, ants and all."
Besides, who knew if there would be another time.

Darcy leaned her head back against the seat and let
the wind from the open car window blow through her
hair. It would look like a haystack by the time they
got to whatever spot Cullen had chosen for their picnic, but she didn't care. She'd made up her mind that
she wasn't going to worry about anything today. Not
the future, not the past, not even the present that was
all tangled up in both of them. Today, she was simply
going to enjoy the moment.

She'd been mildly surprised when Cullen headed
the car north out of Santa Barbara, but when she
asked him where they were going, he shook his head
and said it was a surprise. The idea of a mysterious
destination fit right in with her mood so she simply
leaned back to enjoy the trip.

They were driving up the coast highway and the
Pacific sparkled on their left. A few miles above Santa
Barbara, Cullen turned inland, driving between rolling
hills that still showed green from the winter rains.
Live oaks dotted the land, their heavy trunks and
twisted branches revealing their age. He turned onto
a gravel road, drove a couple of miles and stopped
the car in a tiny valley that nestled between two hills.
As soon as he shut the engine off, silence washed over
them.

"What do you think?" There was a certain tension in his voice as if her answer was important to him.

Darcy looked from him to the emptiness around them. "I think it's beautiful," she said truthfully. "But it seems like a long drive for a picnic."

"I'm going to build a house here." He pushed open his car door and got out. Darcy followed suit. She looked at the site again, visualizing a house cradled against one of the hills, the little valley stretching out from the front door.

"It's a wonderful place for a home."

"I don't want to disturb the site any more than necessary, so it may take a little longer than usual because we won't be bringing in as much heavy equipment."

Darcy came around the car to help him unload the picnic things from the trunk. Cullen continued to talk about his plans for the house as they headed for the shade of an ancient sycamore, laid out a blanket and spread their picnic items along one edge of it.

By the time they'd eaten the sandwiches they'd bought in town, Darcy felt as if she could see the house he'd described. Redwood and glass, a style somewhere between traditional and modern, with plenty of light filling the rooms and a big deck carefully fitted around the existing oak trees. The house wouldn't blend in with its surroundings right away, but in a few years when the sun had weathered the redwood to a soft, faded gray, you'd probably have to look twice to know there was a house there.

"It sounds beautiful," she said wistfully. She drew her knees up to her chest and narrowed her eyes as she pictured how the house would look. "I envy the people you're building it for."

"Don't."

"Don't what?" she asked, still looking out at the imaginary house.

"Don't envy them."

"Why not?" Now she turned to look at him, her brows raised in surprise.

"Because it's us. Or maybe, we're them."

"We're who?"

"We're the people who are going to live in that house." Cullen had been leaning back on his elbows but now he sat up, close enough that his shoulder almost brushed hers. "It's my lot, Darcy, and it's our house I was describing. If you like it, that is."

"If I like it?" She stared at him.

"If you don't, I'll come up with another design."

"No. No, the design sounds perfect." She turned and looked back at the spot where he'd planned to build. The house was still there in her mind's eye, only now it was her house—her's and Cullen's.

And the baby's.

She shivered a little, the image blurring around the edges. He was asking for a bigger commitment than they had now. He hadn't said it yet but the question was there.

"I don't know, Cullen." She shook her head. "It's a beautiful place and the house sounds wonderful but I— Oh."

Her words ended on a squeak of shock as she turned back toward him and saw what he was holding out to her. It was a small black box. A jeweler's box.

Just the size box to hold a ring. Darcy stared at it in shock, her mind spinning. When she didn't reach to take it from him, Cullen brought up his other hand to open it. Nestled on a bed of black velvet was a diamond solitaire, utterly simple, utterly beautiful. Utterly terrifying.

"Marry me, Darcy."

"Oh, God." She lifted one hand to her mouth, still staring at the ring like a rabbit mesmerized by the glare of headlights on a country road. Realizing that "Oh, God" was not exactly an intelligent response to a proposal, she tried again. "Why?"

"Because I love you."

It was the first time either of them had spoken the words out loud and the simple beauty of them made tears well in Darcy's eyes.

"Oh, Cullen. I love you, too."

"Good." His grin was a little crooked around the edges. "That makes the feeling mutual. Say yes and everything will be perfect."

The word trembled on the tip of her tongue. *Yes, she loved him. Yes, she would marry him.* It seemed such an obvious progression.

But it wasn't simple at all.

Darcy scrambled to her feet and turned away from him. She pressed her forearms against her diaphragm, trying to still the flutter of panic there.

"I can't marry you."

"Why not?" Cullen asked calmly as he stood up behind her. "You love me. I love you. What could be simpler?"

"I wish it was that simple but there are things you don't know about me."

"There are things you don't know about me. That's one of the things marriage is for, so you can get to know everything about the person you love."

"No. There are bad things you don't know," Darcy said, her voice so low he had to strain to hear it over the whisper of the breeze in the grass.

"Like what?" Maybe, finally, she'd tell him what it was that tortured her so. He closed his hands around her upper arms, trying to reassure her without words that he was there for her. "Tell me, Darcy."

"I was married before."

Cullen's fingers tightened momentarily in surprise. He hadn't been expecting that. A part of him instantly rejected the idea that she'd ever belonged to anyone else, bound by ties of man and God tighter than any he'd yet claimed.

"That's not a crime," he managed to say calmly. "Are you divorced?"

"Yes," she said indignantly. She pulled out of his hold and turned to look at him. "Do you think I'd be living with you if I were still married?"

"I don't know. You said there were things I didn't know. Being divorced isn't a crime, either." His eyes searched her face, searching for something he didn't want to find. "Are you still in love with him?"

"No! God, no." It was her turn to take hold of him. "I don't love anyone but you, Cullen. I don't think I ever loved him. I was lonely and he seemed kind and…we got married. But I didn't feel anything for him that was even close to what I feel for you."

"I believe you." He felt the knot in his stomach uncoil a little as he drew her close and stroked his hand over her pale gold hair. "You haven't told me anything to make me regret proposing, Darcy. Is that all there is?"

It wasn't her marriage she'd been afraid to confess to, Darcy thought as she pressed her face against the soft cotton of his shirt and felt the reassuring thud of his heart. Her marriage was the least of the secrets she was keeping.

"You can tell me, Darcy."

Maybe she could. If she could tell anyone, it would be Cullen. But what if she told him and then he looked at her the same way Mark had? Mark had promised to love, honor and cherish her, but in the end he'd hated her, blamed her for what had happened. Maybe he'd been right to blame her. She'd managed to survive it when Mark looked at her that way. But if she ever saw the same look in Cullen's eyes, she knew something vital would shrivel and die inside her.

"Darcy? Is there something else?"

"No." She closed her eyes as she whispered the denial. She couldn't take the chance.

"Then there's no reason why you can't wear this," Cullen said, his voice husky as he slid the ring on her finger.

She curled her fingers as if to stop him, but it was too late. Opening her eyes, she stared at her hand where it rested on his chest. The diamond glittered back at her, warm with promise, glittering with hope.

"What about Angie?" she whispered, still staring at the ring.

"We've managed so far, haven't we?"

"Yes, but—"

"Then we'll keep managing."

He made it sound so simple. Darcy moved her finger, hypnotized by the rainbow lights that danced from the ring. Was it possible it really was that simple? And she was simply complicating things unnecessarily?

"Stop trying to complicate things, honey." Cullen's words matched her own thoughts so closely that Darcy wondered if he could actually read her mind. "We can make this work if we want it bad enough."

"I don't know."

"I know." He slid his fingers under her chin and tilted her face up to his. His eyes were so bright and clear that it seemed as if the sunlight was caught in them. "I love you, Darcy."

"I love you, too," she said, her tone more despairing than happy.

"You're going to have to work on that," he chided. "You're not supposed to sound so gloomy about it."

"I'm sorry." She summoned up a smile. "I do love you, Cullen."

"That's better. Not perfect, but better. You'll have years to practice after we're married."

"I haven't said I'll marry you," she protested in a panic.

"You haven't said you won't, either."

Her eyes searched his, wondering how it was possible that she was the only one with doubts. But there was no trace of doubt in his eyes. He looked as if he knew exactly what he was doing. She only wished she felt the same.

"I think it's traditional to kiss right about now," he said lightly.

But there was nothing light about his kiss. The kiss was pure hunger and need. Darcy could have resisted the hunger, but she wasn't proof against the need. Her head was still spinning with doubt as her hands slid into the thick, dark hair at the nape of his neck.

Cullen groaned and crushed her closer still, deepening the kiss to passion. Darcy answered with a passion of her own, her mouth opening to his, welcoming the invading presence of his tongue. The kiss went on and on until she felt almost light-headed from lack of oxygen. They broke apart at last, stepping back to stare at each other.

"Darcy?" He made her name a question. For answer, she reached for the buttons on his shirt.

She didn't notice the roughness of the blanket against her back. All that mattered was the solid weight of Cullen's body above her, the feel of him within.

Lying there in the open with no witnesses but the sun and the wind and a hawk tracing lazy circles in the sky, they confirmed their love in the most elemental of ways. In the final moment, as her body arched taut as a bowstring against his, the sun caught on the ring he'd given her and the resultant rainbow seemed dazzling with the promise of dreams fulfilled. If only she dared to reach for them.

The trip back to Santa Barbara passed in almost complete silence. Darcy alternated staring at the ring on her finger and staring out the window, between elation and terror.

Angie greeted them both with her usual good cheer, clearly holding no grudge for having been abandoned for the better part of a day. Darcy hung back, as usual, watching as Cullen picked Angie up and swung her over his head. There was a familiar ache in her chest, but for the first time she recognized it for what it was. It wasn't a longing for the past, it was a hunger for the present, a need to be part of the picture, a yearning to come in out of the cold.

Though the day's heat lingered on the evening air, Darcy shivered, frightened by the depth of her need. Inside her, a little voice was saying that she didn't deserve to step into the warmth, that she could never make up for her terrible failure.

She was careful to keep her left hand hidden while they chatted with Marie. She wasn't at all sure about her engagement. The last thing she wanted to do was accept congratulations. She was grateful when Cullen didn't say anything to the other woman, but then on the way home she wondered if that had been out of consideration for her or because he was having second thoughts.

But when they went to bed, he turned and drew her into his arms, and he certainly didn't feel like a man having second thoughts. Having burned away some

of the urgency earlier in the day, this time around
their lovemaking was full of tenderness. Soft sighs,
gliding touches, a slow build to a shivering comple-
tion that left them both replete.

"I love you," Cullen whispered against her hair.

"I love you, too."

Darcy lay awake long after he'd gone to sleep.
Staring into the darkness, she realized that she
couldn't marry him without telling him the truth. The
thought sent a chill through her but she knew it had
to be done. She couldn't keep a secret like that for
the rest of her life and it was better that it come out
now, before the ties between them were woven any
tighter.

She tried to tell herself that it would be all right.
He wasn't anything like Mark. If anyone could understand, it would be Cullen. Tears burned her eyes
and wet her cheeks as she stared into the darkness,
the weight of old guilt so heavy on her chest that it
actually hurt to breathe.

God help her, how could she expect anyone to understand that she'd been responsible for her own
baby's death?

It seemed as if she'd barely dropped off to sleep
when the nightmare grabbed her. There was the crib,
all draped in black ribbons. Somewhere a baby
cried—her baby—but she couldn't get to him.
Something held her feet in place. The cries went on
and on and she tried to lift her hands to cover her
ears, but the same force kept her hands captive. She
could only stand there, listening to the crying, struggling to break free.

And then Mark was standing in front of her, his pleasant face twisted with grief and hatred, his mouth an ugly slash, the words spilling out like venom-tipped darts. *What kind of mother are you? This was your fault. Your fault…your fault…your fault…* And then he was gone and the crying stopped and there was only silence. She was free to move at last, but it was too late. She crumpled to the ground, sobbing. She was alone. Alone. Just as she'd always be, just as she deserved to be.

"Darcy! Wake up!" Cullen's voice was mixed with the sound of her own sobs as Darcy swam up out of the depths of the dream. Her fingers dug into the muscles in his arms as she pressed herself against him, drawing strength from his solid warmth.

"It's okay. I've got you safe," he murmured, stroking her hair, holding her until the tremors eased. "That must have been one hell of a nightmare."

Darcy said nothing. She felt the weight of his ring on her finger and opened her eyes to stare at it in the darkness. It might have been her imagination but she thought she could almost see a flicker of light in the heart of the stone. But it was gone in an instant, as if it hadn't been there at all.

Her thinking, which had been muddled from the moment Cullen had said he was building a house for the two of them, was suddenly crystal clear. The dream had been a reminder, a warning. She'd almost let herself forget, almost let herself believe that she could leave the past behind. But it couldn't be done. Some things just couldn't be forgotten. Or forgiven.

"You want to tell me what it was about?" Cullen asked, his hand stroking her back.

"I can't marry you."

His hand froze for an instant. "You mean, you dreamed you couldn't marry me?"

"No. I mean, I can't marry you." Darcy pulled away from him and he let her go without a struggle. She could feel his eyes on her as she slid off the bed and groped for the robe she'd draped over the foot of the bed. She slid it on just as he turned on the lamp next to the bed.

"Why can't you marry me?" He sounded more curious than hurt, but Darcy knew it was because he didn't believe she meant it. But she meant it. She knew what she had to do and this time she wasn't going to persuade herself otherwise.

"I just can't. It would be a mistake." She belted the robe around her narrow waist and ran her fingers through her hair to comb it into a rough sort of order.

"Does this have something to do with your nightmare?" Cullen slid off the bed and she averted her eyes from his naked form, not looking at him again until she heard the whisper of jeans being pulled on and the rasp of a zipper.

"It's not the nightmare." A partial truth, anyway. "I just realized that it would be a terrible mistake if we got married. It wouldn't be fair to you."

"Let me be the judge of what's fair to me," he snapped.

"And it wouldn't be fair to the baby," she continued as if he hadn't spoken.

"I thought we'd settled that issue."

"No. We just postponed it. I know you think we could work things out, but the truth is that I can't be what you want, Cullen."

"You *are* what I want, dammit! Why would I ask you to marry me if I wanted something else?"

"You want a mother for Angie and you think I'll become that if you just give it a little time."

The color that stained his cheeks confirmed the accuracy of her words.

"I'll admit that I've got my fantasies of the three of us as one big happy family," he admitted gruffly, "but if that doesn't work out, that's okay. What's important is that we love each other. Or have you changed your mind about that, too?"

"No. I love you." She bent her head to stare at the ring she'd twisted off her finger. "It's because I love you that I can't marry you. And I can't live with you anymore, either."

"Oh, for chrissake! Don't give me a bunch of psycho babble. You don't *not* marry someone because you love them."

"That's exactly what I'm doing." She tossed the ring onto the bed, where it lay between them. All the life seemed gone from it. It was suddenly just a band of gold with a lifeless rock in it.

Cullen lifted his gaze from the ring to Darcy's face. He was chilled by what he read there. She meant it. She really intended to leave. He drew a slow, steady breath. She was upset. He'd rushed her this afternoon, just what he'd promised himself he wouldn't do. Whatever her demons were, he'd known they couldn't be conquered easily. Obviously the nightmare had shaken her badly. In the morning, when she'd calmed down, they'd be able to talk about this. He'd give her more time, if that's what she needed. But he wasn't going to lose her. Not without a fight.

He bent to scoop the ring off the bed, closing his fingers so tightly around it that the setting dug into his palm.

"It's late. We're both tired. Why don't we go back to bed. I'll sleep on the sofa," he added quickly, seeing the objection in her eyes. "You can't move out in the middle of the night, anyway," he added, striving for a reasonable tone and finding it with considerable effort.

Darcy nodded slowly. "I should be the one to take the sofa, though. It's not big enough for you."

Cullen wondered if it struck her as ironic that she'd just driven an emotional stake through his heart and now she was worried about the sofa being too short. But it probably made perfect sense to her since in her mind she was doing this for his sake, anyway.

"I'll take the sofa." At least that way he knew she couldn't sneak out in the middle of the night because he'd be between her and the front door.

He walked past her but stopped in the doorway and turned to look at her. She stood beside the bed, her arms at her sides, her head bent so that a curtain of pale hair fell forward to conceal her profile. He was hurt and angry and there was a part of him that would have liked to shake some sense into her. But she looked so lost and alone standing there.

Ridiculous as it was, he knew she really believed she was doing this for his own good. In a bizarre way, he supposed this was proof that she loved him. And he didn't doubt that she was hurting every bit as much as he was.

He ran his fingers through his hair, aware that they were not quite steady. When he spoke, his voice reflected the weariness he felt. "Look, I know I rushed you this afternoon. I'm sorry."

"You don't need to apologize." Her voice was so low, he had to strain to hear it. "This afternoon was wonderful."

If it had been so wonderful, then why was she leaving him tonight?

"I thought so, too," he said mildly. "What I'm getting at here is, don't make any hasty decisions. It's late. You're tired. It was an emotional day. You just had one hell of a nightmare. It's not a good time to be making life-altering decisions. Let's sleep on it and we'll talk in the morning."

He waited, but there was no response, unless he counted a faint movement of her head that could have been either a nod yes or a shake no. He chose to interpret it as the former. Not that it really mattered because they were going to talk in the morning, if he had to tie her to a chair to get her to listen.

He sighed. "I'll see you in the morning, then." He turned and left without waiting for a response.

Cullen didn't bother turning on any lights in the living room. Sinking onto the sofa, he set his elbows on his knees and let his head drop forward into the support of his hands. He sat there for a long time, listening to the rhythm of his own breathing and the soft sound of Darcy's muffled weeping from the bedroom.

Chapter Seven

Cullen hadn't expected to sleep at all, but he dozed off sometime around six in the morning, only to be awakened at seven by Angie's announcement that she was ready to get up. Bleary-eyed, he rolled off the sofa, groaning at the stiffness in his back, and stumbled into the nursery. Angie stopped crying as soon as she saw him, giving him that cheery, two-toothed grin that never failed to melt his heart.

"Good morning, imp." She babbled happily in reply, lifting her arms to be picked up.

Cullen changed her and dressed her in a pair of cotton rompers. He carried her out to the kitchen, eyeing the bedroom door as he went by. There was no sign of life behind it. Maybe Darcy was still sleeping. Maybe some sleep would make her see how ridiculous the whole idea of her leaving was.

He fed Angie her breakfast, his attention a little more absentminded than usual. He was just wiping traces of cereal off her hands and face when the doorbell rang.

"Who do you suppose that is?" he muttered as he hoisted Angie out of her seat. Eight o'clock on a Sunday morning wasn't exactly a normal time for drop-in visitors.

"Kiel. What are you doing here?"

"Good morning to you, too." Kiel raised one dark

eyebrow as he walked past his partner into the living room. Cullen shut the door and followed him. "You look like hell," Kiel said bluntly.

"Thanks." Cullen thrust his fingers through his hair and ran a hand over his unshaven jaw. "What are you doing here?"

"Darcy called me." Kiel seemed surprised that Cullen didn't know. "She said you had some things you needed moved. Said it was urgent."

"She called you?" Cullen repeated, feeling as if he'd just been kicked in the gut.

"Yes, I did."

He looked past Kiel to see Darcy standing in the archway that led from the living room to the rear of the condo. She was wearing a pair of jeans and a white T-shirt—one of his T-shirts. Her hair was pulled back from her face in a ponytail, and he was uncharitably pleased to see that she looked every bit as lousy as he felt.

"Why did you call Kiel?" he demanded.

"Because my things won't fit in my car," she answered reasonably.

"Your things?" That was Kiel, looking startled. "Are you leaving?"

"Yes."

"No." Cullen's answer overrode hers. "I thought we were going to talk this morning."

"There's nothing to talk about." Her voice was steadier than he would have liked. She sounded so damned sure.

"There's plenty to talk about." Angie wiggled impatiently, tired of being held when no one was paying any attention to her. Cullen bent to set her on the floor, reaching to hand her a cloth ball to play with. "You can't just leave like this," he said to Darcy as she straightened.

"It's for the best."

"Best for *who?* You? It sure as hell isn't best for me."

"Maybe I should come back later," Kiel said, looking as if he'd like nothing more than to disappear in a puff of smoke. Neither of them heard him.

"You don't understand. I tried to explain."

"Explain? You didn't explain anything. Dammit, Darcy, you can't do this."

"I am doing it." Her voice shook with suppressed emotion. "Someday you'll—"

"If you say I'll thank you for this, I swear to God I won't be responsible for my actions," he snarled.

"Look, it really does sound like you two have things to discuss." Kiel edged toward the door, stepping over Angie, who'd abandoned the ball in favor of exploration.

"Don't go." Darcy took a quick step forward, her hand lifting as if she were a shipwreck victim and Kiel was her last hope of rescue.

"Do go," Cullen said, stepping back to clear a path to the door.

Kiel looked from one to the other, clearly torn. Before anyone could say or do anything, there was an odd sound from Angie, who was sitting on the floor next to the sofa. All three adults looked at her. She looked...odd, Cullen thought. Suddenly afraid, he started toward her.

"What's wrong?"

"She's choking!" Darcy was across the room in a heartbeat and had Angie up and facedown across her lap. Using the flat of her hand, she struck the baby four quick blows across the back. When there was no response, she repeated the maneuver.

Afterward, Cullen could have sworn that he actually heard the pop as the object she'd inhaled popped loose. It dropped from her open mouth and fell to the carpet. There was a moment of utter stillness and then Angie drew a ragged breath. She drew a second and expelled it with a frightened wail.

Cullen sank to his knees, shaking with reaction.

Darcy pulled Angie up and into her arms, rocking her, murmuring soothingly to her as Angie cried out her fright. Kiel bent to pick up the near fatal object and Cullen wasn't surprised to see that his friend's fingers were unsteady.

"It's a button," Kiel murmured, sinking into a chair. "Just a button." He held it out to Cullen.

"I noticed one was missing off one of my shirts a couple of days ago," Cullen said. He closed his fist over the button as if he would crush it. "I thought it had probably come off in the washer."

"A button," Kiel said again, sounding dazed.

Angie's sobs didn't last long. She'd had a fright, but she wasn't hurt and, with no real concept of death or dying, the memory of her fear faded quickly from her mind.

"Here. You should hold her." Darcy's voice sounded thin and her face was almost as white as the T-shirt she wore.

Cullen took the baby from her, closing his eyes for a moment as he felt the wonderful *alive* weight of her. When he opened his eyes, he saw Darcy halfway to the bedroom, her uncertain stride evidence that her knees were no steadier than his. The door closed behind her with a quiet click.

"Maybe you should go after her. She looks pretty shook up," Kiel said.

"Yeah." Angie wiggled to tell him that he was holding her too tight and Cullen loosened his hold. He looked down at her, confirming that she was really and truly all right. Her thick dark lashes were still spiky with tears, but she smiled at him as if she hadn't a care in the world. Which, he supposed, she didn't. He only wished he could forget the terror of the last few minutes as easily as she had.

He stood up and Kiel did the same. "Here. Look after her for a few minutes."

"Me?" Kiel automatically closed his hands around Angie as Cullen thrust her against his chest. "I don't know anything about babies."

"Neither did I," Cullen said over his shoulder.

"But..."

The bedroom door cut off the rest of Kiel's protest. Cullen wasn't worried. He knew his partner would manage. What concerned him now was Darcy.

She was sitting on the edge of the bed, her arms wrapped around herself, rocking back and forth while slow tears seeped down her white cheeks.

"Are you all right?"

She shook her head without speaking, her face

twisted with pain. Moving slowly, Cullen crossed the room and knelt down in front of her.

"You did an incredible job, Darcy. I wouldn't have known what to do for her."

"It was my fault," she said, the words choked.

"Your fault? How do you figure that? It was a button off my shirt."

"All my fault," she moaned, unhearing. "Mark said it was and he was right."

"Mark? Your ex-husband?" It was a stab in the dark but it was obvious that the close call with Angie had triggered some old memories.

"He said it was my fault," she said again, her eyes staring at something he couldn't see. Whatever it was, it was obvious it was tearing her to pieces. Taking a chance, Cullen reached for her hands, prying them loose from where they gripped her elbows and closing his fingers around them, trying to tell her without words that she wasn't alone.

"What did he think was your fault, Darcy?" he asked quietly, wondering if he was finally going to get an answer to the demons that preyed on her.

She blinked and suddenly seemed to see him. He expected to see the shutters come up in her eyes, blocking him out again, but there was nothing but pain and a kind of weary acceptance in her eyes, as if she'd run as far and as long as she could.

"It was my fault our baby died."

Cullen's fingers tightened over hers, his eyes going momentarily blank. A baby? She'd had a baby? He felt as if he'd just received a kick over the heart. He struggled to keep the shock and hurt from showing in his face, but he must not have succeeded.

"I'm sorry, Cullen. I should have told you."

"You're telling me now," he said, his voice steadier than he'd expected. "Tell me what happened."

"We... I guess it never was a very happy marriage," she said in a voice drained of emotion. "We got along okay but there was never really any spark between us. I think we both knew it was a mistake, but then we found out I was pregnant. Things seemed to get better between us and we were happy for a while. Even after the baby was born. Mark was so thrilled that it was a boy."

"What was his name?" His voice was raspy but she didn't seem to notice.

"Aaron. We named him Aaron. He was a beautiful baby. Quiet but happy." She smiled dreamily, lost in memory.

"What happened?" Cullen asked, knowing that if there was any chance of healing, it could only come after the wound was completely exposed.

Darcy's smile faded and her eyes darkened from smoky gray to almost black. "He died. I put him in his crib one night and in the morning he was...gone. Sudden Infant Death Syndrome, the doctor said. He said it just...happens sometimes. Nobody knows why for sure." She sounded almost clinical now, but Cullen could feel her nails digging into his hands where she held him.

"Did the doctor say it was something you'd done?"

"No. But I knew it was. And Mark knew it, too. 'Babies don't just die,' he said."

"But didn't the doctor say that that was exactly what did happen sometimes?" he asked gently.

"Yes."

"Then why don't you believe him? Because Mark said it was your fault?"

"There had to have been some reason," she said fiercely.

"Do you think the doctor was lying to you?"

"N-no," she admitted hesitantly.

"Is this why you don't want anything to do with Angie?" Her hands jerked convulsively in his, but he refused to release them, just as he refused to let her look away from him. "Is it?"

"Yes!" The word exploded from her. "What if it happens again? What if it *was* something I did? And even if it wasn't, what if something else happened? I couldn't go through that again. I couldn't."

She began to cry, not the silent tears she'd shed before but deep, gut-wrenching tears. Cleansing tears. Or at least, that's what Cullen hoped. Standing, he scooped her into his arms and settled down with his back against the headboard and Darcy cradled in his lap.

He let her cry, holding her and murmuring softly to her but not trying to stem the flood of tears. When they'd finally subsided into hiccuping sobs, he handed her a fistful of tissues and waited until she'd mopped her eyes and blown her nose.

"What happened to Aaron wasn't your fault."

"You don't know that," she muttered thickly.

"Yes, I do. The doctor told you it wasn't your fault. If Mark said differently, he was speaking out of pain." It took a considerable effort to speak calmly about her ex-husband when what he really wanted to do was demand his address so he could go and beat him to a pulp. "Sometimes things happen and there's no reason for them. That doesn't mean you stop living."

"What if it happened again?" She sounded like a child, afraid of the dark.

"Are you sorry you had Aaron? Do you wish he'd never been born?"

"No! He was the most wonderful thing that had ever happened to me."

"But you could have saved yourself a lot of pain by not having him," he pointed out.

"But I'd have missed out on so much." Her voice trailed off as the shock of her own words went through her. "I'd have missed out on so much," she whispered again.

"If you try to protect yourself completely, you're not living," he said quietly.

"I don't think I could bear it if it happened again," she said, and they both knew she was talking about Angie.

"It won't. But if something, God forbid, were to happen to her, we'd get through it. Together."

Together. When he held her like this, it was possible to believe that they could get through anything together. She closed her eyes and pressed her face closer against the bare skin of his chest. She felt

Cullen shifting but she didn't open her eyes until she felt him lift the hand that lay against his chest.

"Will you wear this?" The ring looked small in his hand, a fragile circle signifying commitment and promise. "We don't have to get married right away. You can take as long as you want to think about it. And if…if you really feel you have to move out, I'll help you." She could hear how much the words cost him. "But as long as you're wearing this, I'll know that you're still mine."

For answer, Darcy spread her fingers so that he could slip the ring in place. She knew it was her imagination, but it seemed as if the sparkle was back. Hope and promise in rainbow sparks. They lay there without speaking, savoring the feeling of being together— really together this time.

A muffled thud from the living room broke the quiet moment. "I suppose I should go rescue Kiel from Angie," Cullen said. "He looked as if I'd handed him a live bomb."

Darcy followed him from the room, smoothing her tangled hair back. It must be obvious that she'd been crying but Kiel was a good friend. And she wasn't quite ready to let Cullen out of her sight. When he was with her, she believed in the future he saw so clearly, but she wasn't sure the magic would linger away from him.

The look of gratitude on Kiel's face when he saw them was comical. His dark hair looked as if it had been combed with a hand mixer and there was a wildness in his eyes, as if his sanity was starting to crack. He was on his hands and knees behind the arm of the sofa and Darcy assumed he'd been playing peekaboo with Angie.

"She never stops moving," he said, climbing to his feet as Cullen bent to scoop Angie off the sofa. "And she can just about outrun me."

"She can't even crawl decently, yet," Cullen said, giving his partner an unsympathetic look.

"She's still fast," Kiel said darkly. He glanced from Cullen to Darcy. "You two work things out?"

She held up her left hand by way of answer and he broke into a grin. "I take it you don't need any help moving?"

She caught Cullen's questioning look and shook her head. She wasn't moving out. He was right, a life without taking chances was no life at all. Drawing a deep breath, she came forward and held out her arms.

"Let me hold her, please." With a look that combined both pleased surprise and concern, Cullen handed Angie over to her.

Darcy cuddled the baby against her heart. It felt so right to be holding her like this, to let herself feel the love she'd been trying to keep locked in her heart all these weeks.

"Do you think she's old enough to be a flower girl?" she asked, lifting her head to look at Cullen, letting all her love shine in her eyes.

"I think we could set a trend for flower girls in strollers," he said, his voice shaky with emotion.

He put his arm around her, pulling her against his side. The shadows were gone. All that was left was love.

* * * * *

Escape into

Just a few pages
into any Silhouette®
novel and you'll find
yourself escaping
into a world of
desire and intrigue,
sensation and
passion.

Silhouette

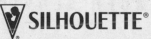

Escape into...
INTRIGUE™

Danger, deception and suspense.

Romantic suspense with a well-developed mystery. The couple always get their happy ending, and the mystery is resolved, thanks to the central couple.

Four new titles are available every month on subscription from the

READER SERVICE™

Escape into...
SUPERROMANCE™

Enjoy the drama, explore the emotions,
experience the relationship.

Longer than other Silhouette® books,
Superromance offers you emotionally involving,
exciting stories, with a touch of the unexpected

Four new titles are available every month on
subscription from the

READER SERVICE™

Escape into...
SENSATION™

Passionate, dramatic, thrilling romances.

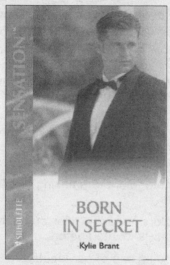

BORN
IN SECRET
Kylie Brant

Sensation are sexy, exciting, dramatic and
thrilling romances, featuring dangerous men and
women strong enough to handle them.

Six new titles are available every month on
subscription from the

READER SERVICE™